The Solution

Even the book morphs!
Flip the pages
and check it out!

Look for other **ANIMORPHS**®
titles by K.A. Applegate:

ANIMORPHS®

The Solution

K.A. Applegate

AN
APPLE
PAPERBACK

SCHOLASTIC INC.
New York Toronto London Auckland Sydney
Mexico City New Delhi Hong Kong

ISBN 0-590-76255-9

12 11 10 9 8 7 6 5 4 3 2 1   8 9/9 0 1 2 3/0

Printed in the U.S.A.   40

First Scholastic printing, October 1998

For Jeff Sampson and all his friends

And for Michael and Jake

The Solution

CHAPTER 1

My name is Rachel.

And I was deep in this strange dream that seemed to involve me trying on dresses at my favorite department store. Only the salesladies kept bringing me things that were way, way too small.

So I said, "Hey, can't you tell these aren't my size?"

And the saleslady said, "Well, we don't have anything in your size."

"What?" I demanded. "You don't have anything in size three hundred and twelve?"

Wait a minute, I thought. *I don't wear size three hundred and twelve.* But at that moment I caught sight of myself in the mirror. And I was in my elephant morph.

I was still growing. Bigger and bigger, till my massive bulk was pressing people against the walls and floors and ceiling.

I looked down, and there, beneath one massive fold of elephant belly, was a small figure in an orange hooded sweatshirt.

"Oh, my God! She killed Kenny!" someone cried.

"Aaaahhhh!" I screamed.

"Try Juniors on the second floor," the saleslady suggested. "Only please don't use the elevator."

And then she leaped at me and started digging her fingernails into me. They were really sharp. So I got mad and I shoved her. Only when I shoved her, she suddenly wasn't a saleslady at all.

She was a bird.

"Aaahhh!" I yelled, sitting straight up.

There, in the darkness of my room, the large gray bird fluttered back and knocked into my desk.

"Tobias?" I whispered. Only it wasn't a red-tailed hawk. It was like a hawk, but gray and white.

<No, it's Aximili. You must come now. Tobias is . . . missing. And Prince Jake is in danger.>

2

I threw back the covers and my bare feet hit the floor. "What?"

<It's David. He is a traitor.>

I was fully awake. Wide-awake and already mad. I grabbed some throw pillows and shoved them under the blankets. Hopefully they would look like me asleep if my mom came in to check on me.

I glanced at the clock. Late. Very late. So late it was early.

I quickly ran through a list of possible morphs. I had to be able to fly. And it was night. I focused my mind on the image of a great horned owl.

I began to change, even as I hammered Ax with questions.

"What happened?"

<Jake, Tobias, and I watched and waited outside Cassie's barn. As you know, Jake suspected David might have decided to turn against us.>

"That weasel! That slimy nyeeerrrrrff."

My tongue had shrunk rapidly in the middle of telling Ax what I thought about David. Probably for the best. Ax would have asked me to define the word I was about to use, and that wouldn't have been a good idea.

I was shrinking all this time, of course. And the brown feathers were appearing on my skin. First as outlines, then as weirdly realistic

3

tattoos, then, quite suddenly, as actual three-dimensional feathers.

<David left the barn in his golden eagle morph. Tobias followed him. We followed soon after, but we could not find either Tobias or David,> Ax explained. <We went to David's home . . . his former home, I should say. We found David there and Jake spoke with him. I do not know what was said. But the Yeerks were watching the house, and a handful of Hork-Bajir attacked.>

<Attacked who?> I demanded sharply. <Jake or David or both?>

<I cannot be sure. But David escaped and Prince Jake followed. He asked me to find you. He said we would need reinforcements.>

<Well, he's got the reinforcements,> I said. <Let's go!>

I fluttered my wings and hopped up to the windowsill. I looked out at a night that was as bright to me as high noon.

I had become a great horned owl. With eyes that looked through darkness and ears that could hear a mouse squeak at fifty feet.

<What about Tobias?> I asked Ax. I certainly hadn't missed Ax's hesitation when he mentioned Tobias.

<I don't know for certain,> he said. <But I fear the worst. David's morph is stronger in the

4

air than Tobias's. And Prince Jake . . . he believes Tobias is dead.>

I felt my insides turn cold. For a few seconds that seemed to stretch into hours, I couldn't move. Couldn't think. I just sat there with my deadly talons squeezing into the soft wood of my windowsill.

Tobias? Dead?

If David had hurt Tobias, I would . . .

But what was the point in making threats? I didn't need to make threats. I *knew* what I would do. So did Jake. That's why he'd sent Ax for me.

at the bottom. And I could make

Eyes that noted...

I felt my muscles...

You could sometimes smell...

David wouldn't...

David is...

CHAPTER 2

I had eyes that saw every blade of grass beneath me. Eyes that noted every small, scurrying rodent hiding in darkness. But I was blind.

All I could see was Tobias. Tobias dead? Not possible!

And David. I could see him, too. Smirking, pouting, easily offended David. David, who half the time seemed to be as reckless as . . . well, me. But other times had been cowardly and quickly panicked.

David, the new Animorph. The one we ourselves had created after David had stumbled across the blue box.

We'd had no other choice. Visser Three had learned that David had the blue box, the Andalite morphing cube. David's parents had been taken, forced to accept the Yeerk slugs in their brains, and made into Controllers.

David's house had been half-destroyed in the battle that resulted. He was known to the Yeerks. His face was burned into the memory of every human-Controller on planet Earth. They would all be looking for him. All searching for the boy who had the morphing cube.

So we'd made David one of us. Using the blue box, we'd made him an Animorph. Capable of absorbing DNA from any animal he can touch and becoming that animal for a period of two hours at a time.

He was supposed to be one of us. And he was, for a while. He was with us on one of our most difficult missions: to rescue the leaders of the free world from the Yeerks.

Sounds impressive, doesn't it? It would have been very impressive, if we'd succeeded. But we had failed.

The leaders of the United States, France, Russia, Great Britain, and Japan were meeting at a secluded beach resort to work out a Middle East solution. It had been the ultimate target for the Yeerks. A chance to make hosts — Controllers — of the five most powerful men on the planet. Or four, at least. One of them — we didn't know which one — was already a Controller.

We had tried to stop them. But we'd gotten ambitious. And Visser Three, leader of the Yeerk forces on Earth, had laid a trap for us.

We'd escaped the trap, but not before David had fearfully agreed to go over to the Yeerk side. Later he'd pretended it was all a ruse. That he was loyal.

Now we knew better.

I flew over dark houses, and over dark parking lots, and over blazing, brilliant, twenty-four-hour stores and gas stations. Ax led us back to the place where he'd last seen Jake and David.

We followed the direction he'd seen them traveling.

Could we find them? And if we did, what would we find?

Suddenly, on the road below us, flashing lights moved swiftly past. A police car. Siren off since it was night, but moving fast. It was moving in the same direction we were.

I looked directly ahead. The mall. It was dark. The parking lot was faintly lit by street lamps at regular intervals. That's where the cop car was heading.

<That way,> I said to Ax.

<Do you see something?>

<No. Just a guess. But that police car is heading there. This is not a bad neighborhood. A

speeding police car could mean we've found Jake and David.>

The patrol car was faster than we were. By the time we arrived at the mall, the officers were driving from entrance to entrance, shining their spotlight and looking for a forced entry.

A silent alarm must have gone off inside the mall. In the distance I could see a second police car racing toward us.

I soared above the acres-large roof of the mall, silent as only an owl can be. I intended to follow the police around the building, but then I saw the skylight. It was a series of glass pyramids built down the middle of the mall to let sunlight into the main section.

One triangle of glass was shattered.

<There!> I yelled to Ax.

We wheeled sharply toward the broken glass. I passed above it and looked down. I could see glittering shards of glass on the landing below. It was hard to tell how bright it was inside the mall, since owl eyes make everything look bright. But it seemed to me that at least a few lights were on.

The question was: What was waiting for me down there? David was an Animorph. That meant he was a dangerous enemy. He had a lion morph, I knew that for sure. And a golden eagle morph.

9

Could I take a golden eagle? No. Not as an owl.

Could I take a lion? No.

And he might be lying in wait. Lying in wait with superhuman hearing and superhuman sight. Not to mention far more than human power.

Well, no matter how good his hearing, he wouldn't hear me. An owl's feathers are specially evolved to make no sound at all as the wind whips across their edges.

<Ax? Are you ready to go in? We'll need to move fast and spread out immediately, just in case he's waiting for us.>

<I am ready,> Ax said calmly.

I spilled air from my wings, changed the angle of attack, and rocketed down toward the jagged hole in the skylight.

Down through the glass! I cleared the reaching, tearing shards; flared my wings; and turned my downward momentum into horizontal speed.

I blew past the marquee for the Old Navy store, barely beneath the ceiling. At first I saw nothing. Nothing but Ax dropping down into view and pulling an identical maneuver going the other way.

But then I saw the broken railing. It was made of thick, tubular steel above thinner, square steel uprights.

All of this bent outward. As if an elephant had run into it.

I turned back and swept my gaze up and down the familiar main mall.

He was lying in a pool of blood. A tiger. Sprawled like he was asleep, but with a shallow pool of black blood extending around his neck and head.

<Jake!> I cried and dropped down toward him.

<Rachel!> Ax yelled. <No! It could be a trap!>

I spread my wings wide and flapped back up, recovering my altitude.

Ax was right. David could be waiting for us to rush to Jake's side. And there could be no possible doubt that it was Jake. Seven-foot-long tigers don't cruise the mall.

<I hear breathing!> Ax said.

I hadn't bothered to listen. I'd assumed Jake was dead. But now I focused all my senses. Yes! There were sounds of breathing. But weak . . . reedy . . . with the sound of blood bubbling with each breath.

<He's unconscious,> I said. <Otherwise he'd demorph. I don't see David. But he could be anywhere. Any*thing*.>

I saw a flash of light, far off down the main

11

walkway. Police lights passing one of the entrances. It would take them a while to get inside. In the meantime they'd surround the mall and watch all the exits.

It would be easy enough for us to get away undetected. But that wasn't what I wanted. What I wanted was David.

CHAPTER 3

<Ax. Demorph.> I felt weird telling Ax what to do. But Jake was down. Not that that meant I was the leader. But I figured someone had to be. We needed to work together.

I felt a slight quiver of doubt. Would Ax do what I asked?

But I could already see the changes in him. He would be fully Andalite soon.

<As soon as you're demorphed, go to the head of those stairs over there. You'll be able to see Jake and cover me.>

It was a large, square opening between floors. An escalator on one end. Stairs at the other end. Railing all around. You know how it is. Basic mall architecture.

I waited impatiently for Ax to demorph. We would need firepower. And very few things were more dangerous than an Andalite.

Ax trotted to the head of the stairs. I began to demorph. I would then morph again and go down the escalator that came from the other direction. I would go down that escalator as a grizzly bear. I didn't think even a lion could do much to hurt me in that morph. And we'd have Jake covered from both sides.

I gradually took on my normal, human shape again. It was so bizarre, standing there in the mall. I was barefoot. Wearing just my morphing outfit, a leotard. I knew exactly where I was, exactly what stores were around me. After all, I spent a good part of my life in that mall.

But this wasn't the mall as I knew it. This was a place of dim lights and deep shadows. Of threat. Of danger.

A sound!

I looked at Ax. We both strained, listening. A ringing sound. Coming from . . . coming from a jewelry store about ten storefronts away.

Staring hard, I could see the broken glass on the floor. Someone had knocked out the window to the jewelry store.

David! Of course. He was probably stuffing a sack full of diamonds right now.

"Go!" I hissed to Ax. "I'll be right there!"

I finished demorphing and actually noticed, despite myself, that Foot Locker was having a big sale. I began to morph again and —

I never heard him. There was no roar. No warning.

I just caught a glimpse of tan reflected in the glass of the Foot Locker store. A low, tan rocket, skimming along the floor.

I spun!

Lion!

He leaped!

I grabbed the bent, twisted railing with one hand and threw myself over the side.

"Aaahhh!" I cried in pain as my wrist and fingers absorbed the weight of my body. I dangled, helpless, swinging above Jake and the floor below. Then I got my other hand to a vertical railing and grabbed on.

But what could I do now?

David shot past and skidded to a stop. It was almost comic. Almost.

If I pulled myself back up, I'd be helpless. If I dropped, I'd break an ankle or leg and be completely helpless.

There were two narrow crossbeams spanning the open space. Banners hung from the crossbeams. I don't know what the banners were about. A sale, maybe, or some special event.

The closest crossbeam was three feet to my left. It was maybe three inches wide. An inch narrower than the balance beam.

I'm an amateur gymnast. But I'd neglected practice for some time. And I'd never tried to swing and then drop onto a three-inch beam fifteen feet or so above a hard, granite floor.

David recovered and came racing back. Ax was still not in sight.

I began to swing wildly, heart pounding the breath out of my lungs.

David came sauntering back, big lion paws silent on the floor, tail swishing, massive, maned head lolling back and forth like some kind of lion version of a way-too-cool dude.

<Alarm clock,> David said. <That's what the Andalite is chasing. I set it.>

I kept swinging. My legs were inscribing a wider arc. I glared at David through the bars.

<All I have to do is bite your fingers, Rachel. Aren't you going to beg for mercy?> David mocked. <Nah, of course not. You're brave Rachel.>

He opened his mouth, turned his head sideways to bite into my fingers, and . . .

I released!

I fell, looked down, saw the crossbeam too far away. One foot hit the beam! I bent my knee and absorbed the impact. I swung my arms over my head, throwing my weight, changing my center of gravity.

For a hideously long moment I teetered back and forth. My other foot jerked and stabbed at the air. Then I felt the crossbeam. I had both feet down!

I breathed for the first time in ages.

David reached a claw through the bars and raked at me. I felt the breeze from his claws.

I stood, motionless, poised, and barely in control.

David glared at me with furious, yellow eyes.

<That's okay,> he said. <I'm not a murderer, you know. I wouldn't kill a human. Now, a bird . . . a tiger . . . sure.>

I stared back at the lion. The traitor. And I said, "Find a place to hide. Because I'll make you a promise: I will kill you, David."

He turned and walked away, laughing as he retreated.

"I'll kill you!" I screamed. "I'll kill you! I'll kill you!"

CHAPTER 4

Ax came running back, just as I was climbing back onto firm ground. I was shaking.

<I heard you shouting,> he said.

"David was here," I said. "He tricked us. We have to get down to Jake and —"

I heard the sound of many voices. The police had gained entry.

I cursed angrily under my breath. "We'll have to hold them off!" I said.

<No,> Ax said. <Jake is unconscious. We cannot move him; he is far too large. Your police will call for medical help.>

I took a deep breath. He was right. "They'll call Cassie's mom. She's the closest exotic animal veterinarian. But what if there are Controllers among these cops? We need to stay with him."

<Agreed. And we must hope he revives within the next hour and a half,> Ax added. <Otherwise he will be trapped in morph.>

Flashlights were playing across the floor down the hall. The police turned away from us, heading toward the JCPenney and temporarily out of sight.

"We have to move fast. They'll be back."

We raced down the stationary escalator and rushed to Jake's side. Up close I could see one of the torn veins in his neck, still pumping slowly, still bleeding. But he was alive, at least. Alive. Unlike Tobias.

<What morph?>

"Flea would be best, but they're almost blind and almost deaf. I want to know what's going on. Morph to fly."

We were halfway into fly morph when new cops arrived and began to walk carefully, cautiously, down the main concourse toward us. They played their flashlights around, looking for . . . looking for they didn't know what.

They were about to get a surprise, that much was for sure.

I morphed as quickly as I could, shrinking

19

rapidly. Jake's already huge orange-and-black bulk seemed to balloon upward, rising above me like a sloped, furry wall.

I felt the gossamer wings extrude from my shoulder blades. I felt the extra legs suddenly sprout from my chest. I felt the painless but still awful melting of my face, the way my nose and mouth ran together, then squirted outward to form the vile, sucking mouthparts of a fly.

But none of these things meant anything to me. Tobias was dead. Jake might still die. And I was going to have to go after David. I was going to have to hunt him down.

I was going to hunt him down and destroy him.

No, not destroy. That was a weasel word. It was vague, meaningless. I was going to kill him.

I felt sick inside. It might have been the morphing that was annihilating my internal organs and replacing them with the primitive organs of a housefly.

Or it might have been the feeling that comes from rage and hate.

<Ax? Tell me something. When Jake sent you to get help, why did you come for me and not Marco or Cassie?>

<Prince Jake was specific. Get Rachel.>

<Did he say why?>

Ax hesitated a moment. Then he said, <Jake

told me Tobias was probably dead. I said this was a terrible thing. And Prince Jake said, "Yes. If David's killed Tobias, we may have to do a terrible thing, too. Get Rachel.">

I don't know how that made me feel. I'm not a person who obsesses over her feelings. You know what I mean? Some people can't stop "looking inward" constantly, and that's not me.

But it definitely made me feel strange. Jake had called for me specifically. Because he wanted someone who would do precisely what I was planning to do.

Like I say, I'm not big on feelings, but something about that felt wrong.

And yet, as I completed the morph to fly, I knew Jake had picked the right person. See, I cared for Tobias. I don't think I even knew how much I cared till right then.

But if David had killed him, I would have revenge. I would make Tobias's murderer pay.

21

CHAPTER 5

I was bathed in light.

A loud, booming, vibrating human voice said, "What the . . . that's a tiger! Frank! That's a *tiger!* In the *mall.*"

"That sure as shooting is a tiger."

"What do we do with it?"

"Call it in to the sergeant. It's hurt. Need to call someone . . . and I'll be racked if I know who. Just keep your weapon on it. It could still be dangerous."

<Ax! Into Jake's ear,> I said.

We hit the start button for our crazy fly wings and lifted off. It took a few seconds, using the fly's mondo bizarro shattered TV set eyes, to find

Jake's ear. But then we spotted a vast, triangular cave.

It was a cave full of long hairs. A cave full of resonating sounds from outside and from the body of the tiger.

<Ax, how long has Jake been in morph?>

<I can only approximate. I believe it has been about thirty-two minutes.>

<About thirty-two minutes? That's your idea of "approximate"?>

<I am assuming he flew straight to this mall from the spot where I left him, and morphed as soon as he reached this place,> Ax said. <It may be as much as thirty-five minutes.>

<Should be time enough for Cassie's mom to get here,> I said.

But Cassie's mom was not the next person to arrive. The paramedics arrived faster. And to my amazement, they went right to work on Jake — once they were sure the tiger was unconscious.

They put pressure on the terrible wound in Jake's neck and slowed the bleeding. But there wasn't much else they could do.

Half an hour later, Cassie's mother arrived. So did Cassie's father. And Cassie herself. Maybe she'd guessed that news of a wounded tiger in the mall meant Jake.

<Cassie! It's me, Rachel,> I called in one-to-one thought-speak.

Of course Cassie couldn't answer. But she could hear.

"Set up for an IV. He's lost a lot of blood," Cassie's mother said in a clipped, professional tone I'd never heard before.

<Cassie, this tiger is Jake. He's been in morph for a little over an hour. You need to get him conscious. It was David. David attacked him. And . . . Tobias. Tobias is . . .> I couldn't say it. I couldn't. <Just, look, get Jake conscious, no matter what. I have Ax with me. We need to go look for David. He may go after Marco next.>

"Wait a minute, I know this tiger," Cassie's mother said. "He's one of ours. He's from The Gardens. No one alerted me there'd been an escape! Okay, now squeeze the bag a couple of times to get the blood flow started. I'm going to close that wound right here and now. He won't make it otherwise."

<Cassie, if you hear me, just say "okay.">

"Okay," Cassie said. "Good luck."

"Good luck?" Cassie's father echoed. "We don't need luck, we have your mom."

<Ax, you ready?>

He said he was, and we flew. No one, with the possible exception of Cassie, noticed two flies emerge from the tiger's ear.

As we flew off, I had to fight the fly's urgent desire to land in the puddle of blood and take a taste.

We rose in our crazy, loopy fly way, and as I skimmed above the heads of the paramedics, vets, and cops, I heard one of the paramedics say, "We figure he fell through that skylight up there. The glass must have cut him."

"That must be it," Cassie's mother agreed. "Only, you know, if I didn't know better, I'd swear this wound was made by another big cat."

"Will he live?" Cassie asked.

I didn't hear the answer. I wasn't sure I wanted to hear the answer.

I set course for the broken skylight. There were cops on the roof of the mall but we found a place to land, out of sight behind a house-sized air-conditioning unit.

We demorphed quickly. I could hear two police officers talking in a low whisper just on the other side of the A.C. unit.

"A tiger, here? With no one knowing it's escaped? It must be one of the Andalite bandits in a morph."

We knew the police force had been partly infiltrated by the Yeerks. Still, it was a shock hearing them talk about Andalites.

"You may be right, but there's nothing we can do about it. None of the other cops here are our people."

"Visser Three won't take that attitude," the first cop said, shivering despite the fact that it was not cold. "He'll think we should have found a way to kill it."

"Then maybe Visser Three doesn't need to hear about this."

"Yeah. No need to bother him with every minor thing that goes on. Yeah. We keep our mouths shut."

Ax and I continued morphing again. He to his harrier morph, me to the great horned owl again.

We flew away into the night in a straight line for Marco's house. Marco would be asleep, unsuspecting. He was safe behind locked doors and strong walls.

Only walls and doors meant very little to an Animorph.

I began to realize just how hard this was going to be. Visser Three had been trying to wipe us out for a long time. He had thousands of human-Controllers, Taxxons, Hork-Bajir, spacecraft, and all of his own bizarre, deadly morphs.

We had just the six of us. Only . . . it was just five now. And maybe four.

Just us, against a person who could become any animal he could touch. A person who could be any living, breathing thing. A flea in your hair, a cat in a tree, a bat in the night, and, when you were unprepared, when you were vulnerable, a lion or tiger or bear.

I was starting to realize why Visser Three hated us so much.

CHAPTER 6

The sun was just thinking about coming up as we approached Marco's house. It was already bright as day to me, of course. But I could tell the difference just the same. The black sky was becoming gray in the east.

I felt like I was boiling inside. Like pressure just kept building up in me. Like I was going to explode.

Too much swirling through my brain. Tobias, dead. Maybe Jake as well. David, a traitor with all the powers of an Animorph.

And at the same time, we had the biggest mission of our lives. The heads of state were still meeting. Controllers, including Visser Three himself, were still conspiring to enslave the most powerful of all humans.

It was too much. Way too much. I couldn't think about all that.

One thing at a time, Rachel, I silently told myself. Priorities: David was number one. Everything else was number two.

David had to be stopped. Before he could stop us.

But still, somewhere in the back of my mind, it bothered me that Jake had sent Ax to get me. Me, specifically. Once he knew that extreme measures might be taken, he said, "Get Rachel."

What did that mean? Was that how Jake thought of me? As some crazed, violent nut who would do anything?

No, of course not. He just knew I was good in a fight. That's all. It didn't mean anything.

Besides, wasn't it true? another part of my mind argued. *Wasn't it true? Wasn't I just the person to call if you needed to kill an Animorph?*

Marco's house. Marco's window. Open.

Open? Did Marco leave his window open? Yes, if he'd already flown out of it. Maybe that was it. Maybe Marco wasn't home, had already left. Maybe he'd sensed we needed him.

But as I wheeled to traverse the back of the

house, bringing myself closer to the window, I saw Marco inside, in bed.

<This smells bad,> I said to Ax.

<You have a strong sense of smell in that morph?>

<I meant *it*, you know, figuratively. Visser Three laid one trap for us. David laid another. I'm done walking into traps.>

<Agreed.>

<Marco!> I called in thought-speak. <Marco! Wake up! Wake up, now!>

I wanted to see him wake up and look around. I wanted to make sure he was alone in the room. He was asleep facedown. He rolled halfway over and gave the blankets a kick.

<Wake up!> I yelled.

Suddenly he sat up and looked around. He scratched his face. Then he looked around again.

<Marco, it's me, Rachel. I'm outside. Are you alone in your room?>

He didn't smile or leer. He just nodded. Yes, he was alone.

<Okay, let's go,> I said.

Ax was ahead of me. He swooped down toward the window. Marco stood watching, smiling almost. His hands were behind his back.

Swoooosh! Ax swooped through the window and —

Marco pulled his hands out from behind his back. The Louisville Slugger swung in a short, sharp arc.

WHAM!

The bat hit Ax square in the face. I saw a piece of shattered beak go flying, twirling away like shrapnel from an explosion.

Ax fell to the grass outside. Marco laughed quietly. I saw his sides shake.

But of course, it was not Marco at all.

David. David had morphed Marco.

Ax lay on the grass, unmoving. Marco/David held up one finger. Then another. Then another. One, two, three.

He was counting how many of us he'd killed.

One, two, three: Tobias, Jake, Ax.

But . . . it should have been four! What about Marco?

Of course! Marco was still alive because Marco had been human. David had said it himself: He would never take a human life. He would only kill animals. A hawk, a tiger, a harrier. Not a human.

As I watched, I saw Marco/David begin to blur. The nose and eyes became subtly different. Now he was just David. But he was still morphing when he stepped back out of sight.

I had to think. David was wiping us out, one

by one. What was his next move? What was his next morph? Jake would know. Jake was the leader, not me.

I had to get to Ax. No! That's what David wanted.

No, I had to get to Marco. The real Marco, who was probably unconscious inside the house.

No, wait, that wasn't right, either.

And then the golden eagle came flapping out of the window. Another of David's morphs.

It was one-on-one. Him and me. Golden eagle against owl. He was faster. Stronger. But it was still mostly dark and the air was cool, with none of the warm lift it would have later in the day after the sun came up and baked the ground.

He was faster and stronger, but the night belonged to me.

I turned and raced away. He followed. Ax lay still on the damp grass. But he was breathing. And to my infinite relief, he was no longer entirely a harrier.

<Follow me, David,> I said. <We'll see who wins this aerial dogfight.>

<Brave words,> he sneered. <But you're mine. Just like that Bird-boy of yours was mine.>

And that's when the pressure inside me evaporated. I was cold again. Cold as a frozen lake. I knew what to do. And I wanted to do it.

I shouldn't resent Jake for thinking of me, I realized. It's what made him a good leader: He knew us all. He knew me.

<For you, Tobias,> I whispered. And I led David toward his doom.

CHAPTER 7

I flew at top speed. But David was faster. His huge wings plowed through the air.

But see, I had an eagle morph, too. I know what eagles can do and what they cannot do. I know it like no human being can possibly know it.

I knew exactly how quickly David could turn, how well he could accelerate or slow down. I knew so precisely what David could see that I might as well have been looking through his eyes.

I wanted him to see me. But he couldn't reach me, not yet. Not until the time and place I had chosen.

Silently I swooped low across rooftops, swerved around trees, swooshed down the shadowed setbacks between homes. I skimmed fences and dropped behind them, out of sight, to suddenly change direction and gain a few feet of breathing room. I shot through gaps in the trees, gaps too narrow for David's vast wings.

But always he kept up. He never gained too much, and I never allowed him to lose me.

<You're very good, Rachel,> he said. <You know, I wish I didn't have to do this.>

<Yeah, but you just can't help yourself,> I sneered.

<You all left me no choice! You forced me. What was I supposed to do? Let Jake order me around, let him get me killed? Spend the rest of my life hiding?>

<What do you want, pity?>

<I lost my family. Everything! Thanks to all of you.>

<What are you, nuts? We're not your problem. Or at least we weren't until you turned against us.>

I was nearing the most dangerous part of the chase. As long as there were trees and buildings, I could take advantage of my smaller size and superior night vision. But now we were emerging over an open field, leaving the houses behind us.

Just a hundred yards or so to go.

David poured on the speed. Those huge wings propelled him after me.

I dodged. But he anticipated my move. He cut the angle and came within two feet of me!

But I could see my target in the night. I could see the high power lines.

Could David see them?

Up, up I went, my wings screaming from the effort.

But now David was all over me. Within five feet of the wires, I felt those wings shadow me.

<Aaaahhh!> Sharp pain, as steel-strong talons sank into the muscles of my back.

<Noooooo!> I screamed in frustration. I stopped moving forward. My wings beat uselessly. I wasn't going to reach the wires. I wasn't going to watch David fry on ten thousand volts.

Talons squeezed harder . . . harder . . . I lost control of the muscles in the back half of my body. One of the talons was sinking through my flesh, trying to reach my heart.

David began to use his wicked, curved beak on me, tearing at the back of my head.

I was losing. The realization terrified me. Not because it meant I would die. But because it meant David would win.

Tobias . . . Jake . . .

David was going to win. My mind began shutting down. *I should demorph,* I told myself. But no, I was too high up. And it was so hard to concentrate. So hard to focus.

David was actually carrying me higher, lifting me up. That way, if I did demorph, I'd fall to my death.

<Sorry, Rachel,> David said. <But after all, birds die all the time, don't they?>

And that's when it happened.

I saw it drop from out of nowhere. Out of the sky. Out of the clouds it dropped.

Wings back, talons raked forward.

It hit David in the back of his head! Eagle feathers flew. David screamed in pain.

And Tobias — yes, *Tobias* — said in private thought-speak, <Rachel, David is really getting to be a pain in the butt.>

David released me. My wings flapped again. I was hurt, but David couldn't know how badly. And he didn't want to fight two at once. He turned and flew away.

<Tobias?> I cried. <But you're supposed to be dead.>

<I am? Who, me?>

CHAPTER 8

Tobias was alive.

It turned out that David *had* killed a red-tailed hawk. And Jake had seen that dead hawk. Only it was a different red-tail.

Tobias had simply lost David early in the evening and had been searching for him ever since.

Jake survived. Cassie found a way to jab a big syringe of adrenaline into him. Enough to wake him up just as her mom was scrubbing up for surgery back at The Gardens.

He demorphed to human and calmly walked out of the zoo. He had to wait two hours for a city bus, but fortunately, Cassie found him a pair of shoes to wear.

Cassie's mother was seriously freaked. Not only had a near-dead tiger simply disappeared. He seemed to have reappeared back in his environment. And there were no signs of any injuries.

Cassie explained that she did a lot of shrugging and kept saying, "I can't believe it, either, Mom. I was only out of the room for a second."

Of course, that tiger was the one whose DNA Jake had originally acquired. Same tiger, but not the same tiger.

Ax was fine. He'd only been stunned. He demorphed, terrified some person driving by, remorphed, and came looking for me.

As for Marco . . . well, Marco awakened to find David standing over him with the baseball bat. He'd been tied up and locked in his closet.

It took him the rest of the night to get loose.

It had been a bizarre night. But the most bizarre thing was that when it was all over, we had to go to school.

That's right, school. On zero hours of sleep.

I was so tired my skin was vibrating. I couldn't believe I hadn't been busted by my mom. I got home that morning just about three seconds before my alarm clock went off. And five minutes later she was banging on my door, telling me to get up and help her get my youngest sister, Sarah, ready for school.

The first few periods I just sat and stared at

the blackboard like someone in a coma. By lunchtime I was reviving a little, but it was mostly hunger keeping me awake.

I sat with Cassie. She'd probably gotten three, maybe four hours of sleep. And I hated her for it. Jake grabbed his tray and sat down with us. Normally, we don't all eat together because we don't want people thinking of us as a clique of some kind. That would be bad for security.

But this time we just didn't care. We were a very tired little group of superheroes. I mean, if Visser Three could have seen us right then, he'd have stopped worrying. We didn't look like we could kick butt on a four-year-old, let alone on the entire Yeerk Empire.

"Hi," Jake said and slumped into his seat.

"Uh," I grunted.

"How are you doing, Jake?" Cassie asked.

"Uh," he said encouragingly.

"Well, this is going to be a perky little group," Cassie said, laughing. "Obviously, we need a Starbucks here in the cafeteria. You two could use some coffee."

"Stop. Talking," I said. I snarled a little. I would have snarled more, but I was too tired.

Of course, Cassie wasn't in the least bit intimidated. "You're so grumpy when you lose a little sleep."

We saw Marco heading toward us. He had no tray. But he was smiling. Well, sure, why not? He'd slept half the night and spent the rest of the night in a nice dark closet.

"Hi, guys, how's it going?" Marco said. He swung his leg over the back of the chair and sat down. Tired as I was, that set alarm bells ringing in my head. Marco doesn't swing his leg over chairs. And Marco doesn't act that perky, even when he's had a full night of sleep.

I guess Jake had the same reaction. I glanced at him, and all of a sudden his eyes weren't glazed and unfocused anymore.

"David, I presume," Jake said harshly.

Marco smiled. And then I saw Marco — another Marco, just starting through the food line.

Cassie was bewildered. She looked from Jake to me. I nodded my head significantly toward the real Marco.

"I'll stop him," Cassie said, jumping up from her seat.

The last thing anyone wanted was two Marcos at one table. There was a joke in there somewhere, but I was too busy to think about it.

"What do you want?" Jake demanded.

David/Marco smirked. "What? No small talk? No chitchat?"

I couldn't morph, not there in front of a whole

41

cafeteria full of yelling, laughing, talking kids. But I could reach for my fork. And I could wonder what the tines would do if they were driven hard enough into — I held on to the fork.

"I asked what you want," Jake said calmly.

"I want the blue box. I found it. It's mine. I want it."

Jake actually smiled. "Now, what do you think the odds are of me agreeing to that?"

Marco/David flushed angrily. "You have no choice, big man. You can't fight me. I have the same powers you have. And I'm smarter than you are, so I'll win."

"There are six . . . I mean, *five* . . . of us," Jake said.

I shot Jake a look. He ignored me. I got the message: No need to tell David that Tobias had survived. The less he knew, the better.

"I want the box," David said stubbornly.

"What for?" I said. "So you can give it as a birthday present to Visser Three?"

Cassie came back and sat down next to David. She managed to move her chair closer to his without being obvious about it. It was deliberate, of course. She wanted him to have to deal with her as a human being, not as an enemy.

David blinked. He leaned away from Cassie. Cassie just gave him her big "understanding" look.

"David, I know you've been through a lot,"

Cassie said in a very quiet voice. David had to lean closer to hear. "I know your life has gone terribly wrong. I know you're lonely. I know you're afraid. And I know that deep down inside you feel very sorry for what happened last night. But you must know that you cannot bargain with Visser Three. He won't give you what you want."

David shot her a sharp, surprised look. So did I.

"What bargain?" I asked.

Cassie took a forkful of her food and chewed it carefully. "Shall I tell them, David, or would you like to?" Getting no answer from him, she sighed and said, "David wants the box so he can ransom his parents. Isn't that right, David? You want Visser Three to release your parents so you can have a home again."

For a brief moment there was something vulnerable on the face David had copied from Marco. But then his eyes hardened.

"That's okay, I don't need the box. I have something else Visser Three wants. See, I know that the Animorphs aren't Andalite bandits. I know their names. Their addresses. I give him you," he said, looking at Jake. "And you," he added, looking at me. "And then, you know what? He can do to you like he did to my parents. And he can get his blue box from you."

David pushed his chair back noisily. He stood up and walked away.

CHAPTER 9

□avid walked away. The real Marco headed toward us, looking about like I felt.

I got up.

"Rachel, what are you doing?" Cassie asked. She put out a hand to grab my arm.

But Jake said, "Let her go."

I followed David's back as he wove through the kids just coming in. In the empty hallway outside, David began to change subtly. He was demorphing. By the time he reached the door to the quad, he was himself again. He must have been close to the two-hour limit to risk it.

I caught up with him as he started to trot across the grass. I grabbed his shoulder and spun him around. I was keyed up, throbbing with barely contained rage.

"You looking for a fight right here?" he asked.

"Why not?" I snapped.

He laughed, a little uncertainly. "You would never morph here in the open."

"I don't need a morph to handle you."

"You know, maybe you forget this sometimes, but you are a girl, Rachel."

"And you're a worm," I shot back. "Want to see who wins that fight?"

"Pretty upset over that Bird-boy, aren't you? What, did you like him or something?" He grinned. "That's it, isn't it? Aww, how sweet. Too bad. But you know, birds have a short life span."

"So do worms."

"What are you doing? Trying to scare me?"

"Nah. I wouldn't want to scare you. I just want to tell you something. You rat us out to Visser Three, we'll know. We have sources inside the Yeerk organization."

He made a snorting noise. "Yeah, right."

"How do you think we knew the Yeerks were moving against the President and the others? How do you think we learned that one of those heads of state was a Controller?"

David looked a little less cocky. I could see the wheels turning in his head as he realized I was telling the truth. We hadn't told David about Erek and the other Chee.

"So see, you sell us out to Visser Three, we will know," I said.

He shrugged. "Big deal. Nothing you can do about it."

"Yeah, you're probably right," I said. "Even if we were warned, we wouldn't last long." I leaned close, close enough to whisper in his ear. "But some of us would last a while, you little creep. Long enough to make sure that your parents . . . well, use your imagination."

He stepped back, drew back his fist, and swung on me. I dodged the blow. I grabbed his head with one arm and jammed the fork against his ear.

I fought a nauseating urge to twist the fork, to make him scream in pain.

"You want a war between you and us, that's one thing. We'll play that out," I said. "But you try and sell us out to Visser Three, and your little family will never get put back together again. Never!"

This time I was the one to turn and walk away.

I was shaking. The muscles in my neck were twitching. Suddenly I had a raging headache. My ears were ringing.

I was exhausted, yes. But it was more than

that. I was high on adrenaline. High on the rush of power and violence.

What had I just done? In all the time we'd been fighting the Yeerks, I'd never made a threat like that. What was the matter with me?

I felt . . . not exactly ashamed. But I knew I never wanted to talk to Cassie about what I'd just told David. Or Tobias. Or even Marco.

And as for Jake, I found myself filled with a terrifying surge of pure, utter hatred for him. I couldn't begin to explain it. But I swear at that moment I hated Jake far more than I did David.

I should have gone back to the cafeteria. I should have told them all what had happened. But Jake already knew, didn't he? Jake, the smart, determined leader, already knew all about me.

And I couldn't face him. I couldn't face what he knew about me.

CHAPTER 10

Jake's parents came back that evening. They'd been out of town helping with a cousin of Jake's and mine. The cousin's name was Saddler. He was an obnoxious kid, but he'd been badly hurt in an accident. Now he was being moved to the children's hospital near us.

His relatives were staying with Jake and his family. But we were expected to help out, too, even though my mom hasn't really gotten along with Saddler's family since my parents' divorce.

I was informed of all this when I got home from school. I said "fine" and staggered up to my bed, hit the pillow facedown, and didn't move.

But as tired as I was, sleep wouldn't come. It was a helpless feeling. Being so exhausted and so unable to sleep.

My brain kept buzzing away, like I'd consumed six pots of coffee or something.

I kept wondering: Had I always been like this? Back before the Animorphs, back before that encounter with a dying alien who changed our lives, who had I been?

I tried to remember, but it wasn't like I was thinking about myself. It was like I was remembering some girl I used to know. Like she was an acquaintance I'd forgotten about until someone reminded me. It was like, "Oh, yeah, Rachel. I remember her."

I'd been very into gymnastics, I knew that. Shopping. I guess I'd never exactly been a happy-go-lucky party girl. But I tried to imagine myself back then, and tried to imagine grinding the tines of a fork into someone's ear while I threatened his family.

I almost laughed. It was crazy. I mean, I'm not someone raised in an abusive family or anything. Yeah, my folks got divorced, but probably a third of the kids in school have divorced parents, and another third wish their parents would divorce.

I'd never had to wonder if my parents loved

49

me. I knew they did. They told me. And they showed me.

I wasn't on drugs or anything. But somehow, someway, I had gone from being this occasionally sharp-tongued girl, to being . . . well, as Marco would say, Xena: Warrior Princess.

What made me feel stupid was that I hadn't realized I was changing. But everyone else obviously did. Jake did. When he knew it was coming down to kill-or-be-killed with David, he'd sent Ax to get me. Not Marco. Not Cassie. "Get Rachel."

And in the cafeteria he had let me go, knowing what I would do. Afterward, I'd seen Cassie in sixth period. She didn't ask me what had happened. She didn't ask me what I'd said to David. She'd known.

I could have said, "Look at all the battles I've been through." It would have been a good excuse. Except that Cassie'd gone through the same battles. And Marco. And Tobias.

Would Tobias have done what I did? That was the killer question, see. Because Tobias lived life as a predator now. He'd have every excuse in the world. But I wondered if even he would have gone as far as I'd gone.

And, I wondered something else. What if David ignored my threat? Would I . . . could I . . .

"Rachel! Phone! What are you, deaf?"

I jerked upright. It was dark outside my window. "What?" I asked for no particular reason.

Jordan, my younger sister, stuck her head into the room. "It's Jake. He's on the phone."

I sat up. My head was buzzing. I rolled over and grabbed the phone. "Yeah?" I said, pushing my hair more or less into place.

"It's time," Jake said. "That little extra-credit project we've been working on. It's time for us to give it another shot."

"Oh. Yeah. I'll be right over. Soon as I, you know."

Man, I was stupid from lack of sleep. We still had a mission. We'd failed yesterday evening and had almost been trapped by Visser Three.

Yesterday? Had it really only been yesterday? It seemed impossible, with all that had gone on.

I splashed cold water on my face and ran a comb through my hair. Then I went downstairs to face my mom and try to think up a good excuse why I had to go over to Cassie's house.

"Rachel!" my mother said as she spotted me coming down the stairs. "Good. I need you to watch Sarah. I'm going over to the hospital to be with Saddler's mom and dad."

I was about halfway ready to say, "Fine. That sure beats trying yet again to bust into some heavily guarded compound and getting our brains beat in."

51

But that wouldn't do. "You want me to baby-sit for Sarah and Jordan?"

"No one *baby-sits* me!" Jordan said hotly.

"Oh, yeah?" I mocked. "You are either the *baby-sitter* or the baby-sit*tee*. And you are a baby-sit*tee.*"

"Mom! No way! I can take care of Sarah!" Jordan protested.

"Come on, little babies," I added for good measure.

Well, you can guess where it went from there. Ten minutes later I was out the door. And ten minutes after that I was demorphing inside Cassie's barn.

Everyone else was already there. Ax, Tobias, Jake, Cassie, and Marco. At least, I assumed it was Marco and not David in morph.

"Marco," I said, once I had demorphed. "You know you're a toad?"

"Kiss me and I'll become a prince," he said without hesitation. "I'll be The Prince Formerly Known As Toad. You know you want me. You can't help it. After all, you're a female and I'm . . . well, I'm me."

"Yeah, that's the real Marco," I said dryly.

Cassie laughed. "Believe me, we all did the same kind of thing. I asked him to tell me what it was like when we morphed trout. Just to test his memory."

"And I answered that it wasn't bad except that the cracker-crumb coating chafed a little and I was allergic to tartar sauce. Now can you all stop playing that game? I'm afraid I'll miss a punch line and Rachel will morph to grizzly and eat me before I have a chance to say anything."

"Okay, down to business," Jake said. He sent Ax a significant look and jerked his head toward me.

<Prince Jake would like me to tell you that we are operating under the assumption that David may be here in the barn,> Ax said in private thought-speak. <He is concerned that David may be here in insect morph, listening to our plans. So our plans will be different than we are discussing here.>

I gave a very slight nod. Of course. I'd forgotten. David was one of us, at least in terms of his powers. But Jake hadn't forgotten.

Jake outlined a plan that was basically the same as our previous attempt to infiltrate the banquet at the resort. There were differences, just so it would sound convincing. And we all raised various objections, just to sound even more convincing.

But it wasn't till we were morphed and flying away that Jake told me what he really had in mind.

<Oh, Rachel's gonna love this,> Marco said with a laugh.

He was right. The plan was outrageous, insane, out of control, and violent.

And heaven help me, I liked it.

CHAPTER 11

It was a Marriott resort by the ocean. It had been taken over for a summit meeting by the President of the United States, the prime minister of Great Britain, the premier of France, the president of Russia, and the prime minister of Japan.

Was there security? Oh, yeah. There was security. There were more guys in dark suits and sunglasses with microphones in their ears than had ever come together in one place before. It was like an international Secret Service convention.

That was bad enough. But what was worse was the fact that some of those security guys were Controllers. Some of the U.S. Secret Service, for sure. Probably some of the French, British, Russian, and Japanese, too.

And we knew Visser Three was there, doing everything within his twisted, evil imagination to make Controllers of all these powerful men.

We also knew that at least one of the heads of state — we didn't know which one — was already a Controller.

So basically, this was a tough target. Even for us. There were just way too many guys looking to shoot anything suspicious.

It was also a mission we had to do. Period. Had to. If the Yeerks made Controllers of these guys, that was it. Game over.

We had tried a subtle approach. We'd walked into a trap.

Now Jake was ready for the less-than-subtle approach. This would be like when you're in a chess game and you know you're going to lose so you grab the board and throw it across the room.

That was the plan.

First stop, The Gardens. I was all set on morphs. But Tobias, Cassie, Ax, and Marco needed something new for their night's work.

We needed morphs that could make a big mess. And morphs that could take getting shot by handguns. We all needed what Jake and I already had.

Once that was done we flew straight out to

sea as seagulls. It was a tough flight. The wind was getting stronger by the minute, racing in across impressive waves. And then the lightning started.

<Yaahh!> Marco yelled as the first jagged bolt lit up the clouds and the waves.

It was one bolt, a long pause, then another. Another pause, and suddenly it was as if a light show had begun. Bolts of lightning that looked as thick as trees pushed their jerking way across the sky. Huge bolts struck the waves again and again all around us, even though we were only a few hundred yards from shore.

And the thunder! Imagine the loudest thunder you've ever heard, then multiply it by five. It was like my head was stuck inside a steel drum and someone was hitting it with sledge hammers.

Lightning, thunder, and then the rain began to pour.

<That's nice,> Marco said. <That's just perfect.>

<Jake, we're not going to make any more distance against this wind,> Tobias said. <Especially not with wet feathers.>

<Yeah, you're right,> Jake agreed. <We'll swim the rest of the way along the coast.>

<No problem. All we have to do is land in the water,> I said.

<Seagulls land in water all the time,> Cassie pointed out. <Although maybe not in the middle of a hurricane . . .>

No doubt she was right. But seagull or not, let me tell you, it was a fairly terrifying experience.

Here's the thing. You're a small, white bird. Smaller than an average chicken. The ocean is black as coal, aside from the pale phosphorescence as some of the waves crest. You basically can't see the waves at all because the clouds are totally covering the moon and the stars. But every few seconds the entire seascape is lit up by lightning. Sometimes it's a dim sort of light cast by some far-off bolt whose thunder takes ten seconds to reach you. Other times the lightning is closer, and then the waves are turned into brilliant silver slopes and black, triangular shadows, just long enough to let you realize how tall the waves are.

I floated down, following Jake, for once not rushing out ahead. I have a lot of respect for the ocean.

I almost had to fight to go lower, the wind was so strong.Thirty feet up . . . twenty feet . . .

Lightning!

Suddenly the water was no longer twenty feet below me. It was rushing straight up at me. It was like being in a plane and flying over a mountain, only suddenly the mountain swells up like a zit about to pop and up it comes while all you can do is wait for it.

PLOOSH!

Water foamed over me. But I bobbed easily to the surface, like a cork. I almost laughed. It was easy! I was too buoyant to sink. As I tucked my wings back, it felt just like bodysurfing.

We landed yards apart, of course. There was no way to be more precise. I caught lightning glimpses of the others, tiny white birds riding big black waves.

<Everyone down okay?> Jake called out.

One by one, we answered.

<Okay, now the tough part.>

He didn't have to explain. We all knew. We were going to morph to dolphin. Once we were dolphin, everything would be fine. Dolphins *own* the ocean.

But to get to dolphin, we'd have to become human again. And maybe a seagull or a dolphin belonged out in these two-story waves, but no human being did.

CHAPTER 12

<This is going to be rough,> Jake said. <Everyone be very careful.>

<Jake, why don't we do this one at a time?> Cassie suggested. <I'll go first. Then I can help the others.>

<Okay,> Jake said. <Cassie morphs first. She's fastest.>

It made sense. Cassie was the best at morphing. Jake was using her for her special talent. Like he used Marco for his suspicious mind. Like he used Ax for his knowledge of all things alien. Like he used Tobias for his raptor eyes and ears.

Like he used me. For what? For my recklessness? For something dark that lived inside me?

Cassie's thought-speak voice fell silent as she

began to morph. I saw her only once in a one-second burst of electric light. She was a twisting, misshapen mess of waterlogged feathers and skin with an eerie, Halloween face.

I heard her yelp in surprise and when next the lightning flashed, all I could see was a human hand raised above the water.

<Cassie!> I cried. <Cassie!>

No answer! She was drowning. Stupid to let her go first. She was a great morpher, but I was a better swimmer. I began to demorph as fast as I could.

<Jake, she's drowning!> I yelled.

<Don't do anything stupid, Rachel. She'll pull it out.>

I thought *bull,* but I kept quiet and continued growing, heavier and heavier, less and less buoyant. Soon I was a fifty-pound mass with a handful of feathers. I began to sink. I sucked at the air and filled my lungs, just as a wave crashed down and buried me.

I expected to bob right back up. But the wave had driven me down. And I had no hands to swim with! My feet were huge bird claws, only now beginning to web up.

Panic!

No, no! I ordered myself, enraged by my momentary terror. *Keep morphing! It's the only way.*

But my lungs were burning already. I'd gone

from tiny seagull lungs to human lungs and there wasn't an ounce of air in my body.

I craned my head back to look up. But was it up? I couldn't be sure. It was dark all around me. Dark, as if I'd fallen into a vat of ink. Where was up?

I was swimming now, kicking with human feet and snatching at the water with human hands. But I couldn't feel gravity. I couldn't tell if I was rising or simply plowing myself further and further down.

And then something bumped against me. I couldn't see it, but I could feel rubbery skin.

<Relax, Rachel,> Cassie said. <You're going the wrong way.>

She pushed her dolphin nose under me and propelled me up and up — had I sunk that far? — till my face exploded upward, passing from black water into falling rain.

I swallowed air, swallowed water, slipped back under when a wave took me, then was lifted once more into the air.

I realized I was straddling the dolphin's back. I sagged forward and hugged Cassie's back. "Thanks," I managed to gasp.

<Take a minute. When you're ready I'll keep you above water till you're dolphin enough.>

Ten minutes later we all had morphed to dolphin. Cassie supported me, then she and I supported Jake. The rest morphed quickly after that. Tobias went last. He had to pass through red-tailed phase, so we all worked to keep him above water.

<Great weather for this,> Marco grumbled. <What is this, a hurricane? It's not bad enough being a half-bird, half-human trying to swim. We gotta do it in the middle of a typhoon?>

<Water,> Tobias said darkly. <See, this is what happens. Water is always trouble. Up in the sky you can at least see what's going on.>

<And yet all the worry I felt seems to have evaporated,> Ax said. <I feel . . . quite relaxed. Happy, even.>

<Dolphin brain,> Marco said.

It was true, of course. It's very hard to stay upset when you're in dolphin morph. A dolphin in the ocean is like a kid in a candy store. Like Cassie at a nature preserve. Or like me at a department store sale.

<Well, we're all alive, so let's get going. We're already probably late,> Jake said.

<Approximately ten minutes behind the schedule we discussed,> Ax said.

<Let's motor,> I said.

We took off, a happy, contented pod of dolphins, slipping in and out of the water. We plowed through the almost vertical walls of advancing waves, suddenly going airborne out the back sides.

Storm? What storm? Waves? Waves were fun! Darkness? Who cared? We could echolocate. Wind? It was cool. It could make you soar further when you jumped. Thunder? Just a noise.

As for lightning . . . well, if you swim underwater and you roll onto your side so you can point one eye straight up, the lightning becomes this huge flashbulb. The entire surface of the water flashes brilliant silver, but it's a twisted, mottled silver, like a platter someone has battered with a hammer.

One eye up to the lightning, one eye down into darkness. It didn't bother the dolphin brain. The dolphin brain didn't really have the emotion of fear. Maybe other creatures knew fear, but the dolphin brain was not programmed for it.

Unless, of course, I suddenly saw a black-and-white pinto pony pattern. That would mean a killer whale. And then the dolphin instinct for survival would kick in.

But towering waves? Lightning? Howling wind? Black water? They meant nothing to me.

We ran along the coast till a leap in the air revealed the far-too-familiar lights of the Marriott resort. And now my human mind came back full force, with all its own fears and rages.

See, we weren't done morphing in the water. And this time it would be in the surf.

CHAPTER 13

We echolocated a submarine about a mile offshore. *Dangerously close,* I thought. And of course we were very aware of a number of fast Coast Guard patrol boats cruising up and down through the surging sea.

They played searchlights over the water. But naturally, it was child's play for a dolphin to avoid them.

They disappeared at last behind a small, rugged island about a mile offshore. It was nothing but a jumble of rocks, really. Plus a couple of scruffy trees. I popped up out of the water to get a better look. I didn't know why, then, but something about that desolate place made me edgy.

Or at least as edgy as you can get while you're a dolphin.

We swam toward shore, the six of us abreast. I could echolocate the rising slope of the seabed. It was only a few feet deep and even the dolphin brain was nervous as we felt the waves crashing down and almost slamming us into sand and gravel and broken shells.

<Are we close enough?> Marco wondered.

<We need to get as close as we can,> Cassie said. <A little more.>

Soon my gray rubber belly was scraping the sand and my tail was almost useless.

<Okay, now,> Cassie said. <Our morphs should be able to power up out of this depth.>

I began to demorph. I wasn't looking forward to it. This was practically Hawaii-sized surf. The waves gained power as they came rushing up the sloping seabed. All that water just kept piling higher and higher till it was a rushing, teetering, two-story wall of water.

I tried to time it, but there was no way. A wave caught me mid-morph and slammed me face-down into the sand. Worst of all, we could not allow ourselves to be washed up onto the beach. The beach was crawling with security patrols. Guys in night-vision goggles who saw everything as though it were illuminated by a green sun.

We could not be seen till we were ready. For that reason the surf was perfect. For every other reason, it was definitely not.

I made it to human morph and was nailed by a wave of exhaustion almost as devastating as the real waves. Morphing wears you out. Morphing repeatedly on no sleep is beyond exhausting.

I swear I could have just lain down in the water and fallen asleep. But then I was propelled almost headfirst into the wet seabed.

I fought my way back up and grimly set about morphing yet again.

Now things began to change for the better. I was morphing an African elephant. Tons of African elephant. As I passed my first ton, I found the surf didn't bother me quite as much.

I backed further out to sea to conceal my growing bulk and keep the very recognizable elephant head silhouette from being seen onshore.

I looked left from one eye and right from the other. I saw the rest of my friends growing vast and bulky in the surf.

Jake was in his rhinoceros morph. Marco had chosen to acquire that same animal. Cassie, Tobias, Ax, and I were a matched set of elephants.

The elephant and rhino morphs had several things in common. They were faster than they looked. It took more than a handgun to knock them down. And people who saw them coming had a tendency to want to run away.

We were, I don't know, maybe fifteen tons of bone and horn and tusk and muscle.

<Ready?> Jake asked.

<Ready,> Marco answered.

<This animal's nose moves quite delicately,> Ax said.

I could see fairly well with the elephant's eyes, unlike Jake and Marco, who were half-blind. I could see the softly lit bungalows just off the beach. I could see the taller, brightly lit hotel building beyond.

Our goal was the bungalows. They housed the world leaders. Our plan was painfully simple. If we couldn't stop the Yeerks by subtle means, we'd just tear the place apart. Then, most likely, the big banquet where Visser Three hoped to strike would be canceled.

Like I said, not a brilliant plan. But you know what? As tired, mad, scared, annoyed, worried, and filled with self-doubt as I was at that moment, the sweet simplicity of it all seemed like pure genius to me.

<Hey, Marco, who's that comic book charac-

ter who's always yelling, "It's butt-kicking time"?> I asked.

<That's the Thing. And what he says is, "It's clobberin' time.">

<Yeah? Well, whatever. Let's go do some serious stomping!>

CHAPTER 14

You almost had to feel sorry for the Secret Service and all the other security guys on the beach, huddling in the rain beneath their ponchos while they gazed through night-vision goggles. One minute it's nothing but waves and lightning. The next minute it looks like a small pod of whales has decided to get up out of the ocean and go hang out on the beach.

I mean, their training must have prepared them for almost anything. But not, definitely *not* for the possibility that two rhinos and four African elephants would come trumpeting and snorting out of a one-hundred-year-storm surf.

"Hhhrrrreeeyyaaahhhh!" I announced myself.

I heard a human voice say, "What the —?"

I broke into a charging run. I had to deal with a little bit of a slope, but I had plenty of power and legs the size of tree trunks.

I raised my trunk high and bellowed again.

"Hhhrrrreeee-uh!"

I was running full tilt. So were the others. Suddenly, the lightning flashed and I could see half a dozen utterly baffled men and women in drenched rain slickers, staring at us with six identical open mouths.

Only one reacted like he had a clue. He drew his gun and started firing. Right at me.

BLAM! BLAM!

You'd think a trained marksman could hit an elephant. But I guess it isn't all that easy in a pitch-black night with rain in your face.

Chances were the guy who was firing at me was a Controller. A normal human's first thought would not be to shoot an elephant on the beach.

I went at the man, full speed.

BLAM! BLAM!

The muzzle flash was like tiny echoes of the lightning. This time I felt a bullet hit me in the shoulder. It didn't hurt, exactly. I was just sort of aware of it.

He didn't get a chance to fire again. I lowered my head, bringing my hugely long tusks into line with the gunman, and he turned and ran.

<Remember, we have to assume these are all innocent humans,> Jake said.

His thought-speak voice came to me just as I was considering whether I should run the guy through with my tusks or trample him. Of course, Jake was right. These were innocent bystanders. Mostly.

We were here to wreak havoc and scare the heck out of everyone, but not to hurt anyone on purpose.

Now other guards had decided they'd better shoot at us, too. All down the beach came the sound of gunfire, along with shouts and cries that were instantly snatched away by the howling wind.

<Everyone ready?> Jake called. <Charge!>

Marco laughed. <*Charge?* I bet he's always wanted to say that.>

We charged. Like some mondo freak-o version of Gettysburg, we raced up the beach toward the two closest bungalows.

Fifty yards!

Twenty yards!

I was eating up the beach, my big round feet plowing deep with each step.

A line of bushes. I barely registered thorny scrapes on my gray leather hide.

I was huge! I was a tank! I was running at full speed, my sail-like ears flapping in the wind, my powerful trunk trumpeting madly, my tusks thrusting, searching for something to impale.

I was pure power, pure momentum, pure out-of-control animal energy.

I tore through a decorative trellis and stomped it to toothpicks. Then, a wall! I ran, slewed my head to the side, and slammed that wall with my right shoulder.

WHUMPF!

Crunch!

I backed up a step and swung my weight forward again.

WHUMPF!

Crrrrrunch!

<One more time!> I cried, laughing idiotically in my head. I backed up and this time there was no "whumpf!" just a tearing, breaking, twisting sound. All of a sudden, bright light shone out on me from the big hole I'd made in the wall.

Then I saw Marco in his new rhinoceros morph plow into and through the door. "Into and through" being all one motion.

The security guys were getting serious. Elephants and rhinos running around — well, that was almost funny. Elephants and rhinos beating in doors and knocking down walls — that was a whole different matter.

I shoved at the hole I'd made and found myself blinking in the bright light. Blinking and staring at Marco, and at the man sitting in an easy chair wearing a tuxedo shirt, a tie, black socks, and glossy black shoes. His tux coat and pants were draped over a chair. He had a somewhat familiar face. The leader of a great power.

He was sitting in his Jockey shorts and calmly pouring a glass from a bottle of clear liquor. Then he glared belligerently at me and Marco.

Now, I'm not going to say who this man was, or what nation he headed, but he was drunk. Drunk, but no coward. He just sat there in his underwear, glaring at us, defying us.

<What do we do?> Marco asked me.

<I guess we go tear up someone else's bungalow,> I suggested. Suddenly about twelve security guys came bursting into the room, guns drawn. And not just handguns, either. These guys had automatic weapons on us.

But the man in the chair said something loud and curt in a foreign language. No one fired. The man in the chair made a sort of "after you" sweep with one hand, indicating that maybe Marco and I should leave.

So we did. We went out through another wall and dragged half the roof down with us, but we left.

Behind us I heard a loud roar of delighted laughter. Like we'd really made the old guy's day.

I guess if you think about it, hanging out with a bunch of politicians talking about peace must be kind of dull. After a couple days of that, maybe you kind of welcome massive, enraged animals barging through your living room.

CHAPTER 15

We headed back out into the rain, which was now coming down so hard we might as well have been back in the ocean.

It was chaos!

Spotlights were shining down from the top of the hotel, sweeping madly here and there. There was the pop!pop!pop! of gunfire. There were men in dark suits racing back and forth, guns drawn. There were guys in tuxedos and women in formal gowns running and tripping and yelling. I heard helicopters chopping the air overhead.

And through it all galumphed elephants and rhinoceroses, banging into anything we could bang into.

The thunder was rattling windows. The rain was turning everything to mud. And every few seconds, the lightning would flash and I'd see the entire madhouse scene frozen by the strobe light.

It would have been funny. If people weren't shooting at us.

I targeted the next undamaged bungalow and called to Marco. <Hey! Knock that door down. I'll come right after you.>

<What door? I can't see that far.>

<Veer left,> I instructed. <Okay, go go go! Left!>

WHAM!

<That was no door!>

<I told you left,> I said. <Never mind, I'll finish it.>

I slammed the hole in the wall that Marco had started. This time it went down easier. Two hits and the wall collapsed inward.

BLAM!BLAM!BLAM!BLAM!

Four bullets hit me in the head. I felt them as hammer blows.

I backed away from a phalanx of disciplined, determined-looking men. There were three of them. Behind them, looking mystified, was the most powerful man on Earth.

I swear I had to fight down this ridiculous urge to say, "It's an honor to meet you, sir!"

But blood was flowing down my face and I was feeling dizzy. The bullets had done some damage.

I backed up, dragging bits of plaster and pieces of splintered wood with me. I backed up into a soldier sliding down a rope that seemed to drop out of the sky. I could hear the helicopter directly overhead. More ropes coiled down and more black-uniformed men slid down.

These guys were armed to the teeth. It was time to leave.

<Jake!> I yelled into the darkness. <Jake! The reinforcements are coming in!>

<Time to bail!> Jake yelled to everyone. <Everyone back to the beach!>

Brahahahahahahahahat!

Automatic weapons were firing. I felt my left rear leg catch fire. At least that's what it felt like.

I staggered back and the injured leg almost collapsed. I was hit, and badly.

<Come on, Marco, let's get out of here!>

<But I didn't even get to see the President,> he complained.

<Marco, this really isn't the time.>

We turned and crashed back through the trellises and shrubbery and out onto the windswept, soggy beach.

A human staggered in front of me. He was

mud-smeared and ankle-deep in wet sand. And he was furious. Tony, the White House protocol chief. Except that we knew Tony had been acquired by Visser Three as a morph.

And judging by the screamingly enraged look on "Tony's" face, this was Visser Three.

For a frozen instant, we locked eyes. He knew what I was. I knew what he was.

<I guess we can assume the banquet has been canceled, Visser,> I said. <Now, let's see how fast you can run!>

I went for him, but I stumbled. I was in worse shape than I'd realized. He scampered back, realizing I couldn't catch him. He bounced up and down with rage, shouting, "I won't kill you when I catch you, Andalite! I will make you beg for death!"

No time to sit and exchange pleasant conversation. Besides, we weren't even supposed to talk to Yeerks. We didn't want them realizing we weren't Andalites.

Down the sand I saw the others, some staggering, some seemingly unhurt. I left Visser Three ranting and raving and took off on three good legs. We ran for the water's edge, bullets whizzing after us, and plowed into the surf.

I began demorphing instantly, even as I continued to motor out against the waves. Demorphing would save my life. The bullets should drop harmlessly away, but even if they didn't, all the damage they'd done would be repaired.

I was giddy. I was going to survive! I was laughing, laughing at the sheer, insane rush of it all. No weariness now, just mad, frantic glee at having escaped alive.

<How will they ever, ever explain that?> Tobias wondered.

<I don't know,> I said, <but that's one summit meeting no one will forget.>

CHAPTER 16

I was demorphing to human as fast as I could. As dangerous as it was, the weather probably saved us at this point. The Coast Guard boat had come in closer, but there was no way it could get right in to shore, not with those waves.

I demorphed to human and could feel the injuries fading away, the bullet lead dropping harmlessly to the bottom of the sea.

Once again, I was half-drowned by the time I'd made it safely back to dolphin morph. But I almost didn't care. The after-action depression was starting to set in. The special brand of weariness that comes when all the adrenaline has begun to wear off.

The dolphin mind rescued me. It was as irresistibly happy as always. The DNA of its instincts was reconstituted, fresh with the morphing.

I kicked my gray tail and felt my rubber skin slide easily, confidently through the water. I dove beneath the huffing, chugging Coast Guard cutter and headed out to sea.

And that's when it happened. I fired an echolocation burst, a series of fast, ultrahigh frequency sound waves. The sound waves traveled through the water and bounced back from anything they hit. It was like sonar. Underwater radar.

Then I saw in my mind the outline, the shape. The shape that was imprinted in the deepest DNA archives of the dolphin brain.

It was long. Maybe twenty feet. It was vast, perhaps ten thousand pounds. From its back a long, almost straight dorsal fin rose. The echolocation did not show color. But I knew that when it got closer I would see a black-and-white pattern.

<Killer whale!> I yelled.

It was coming toward us. Its speed was incredible! Something that big shouldn't be able to move so fast.

It was coming for us, and we were helpless. It was faster, more powerful, far, far more deadly. We were more agile, but I knew one thing for sure: It was killer whales who ate dolphins, not the other way around.

<I have it on echolocation,> Cassie agreed tensely.

<What is this creature?> Ax asked.

<It's actually a species of dolphin,> Cassie said. <A close relative of this species we've morphed.>

<Yeah, close relative,> I muttered. <Like Chihuahuas and Dobermans are close relatives.>

<There's just one,> Cassie said. <Strange.>

<Why? What's strange?> Tobias asked.

<Just that orcas usually hunt as a pack,> Cassie said.

<Yeah, well this one is hunting us all by himself,> Tobias said. <Big as he is, he won't need any help!>

<What do we do?> Marco asked.

<He's just a killer whale,> Jake said. <We have human intelligence as well. We can't outfight or outrun him. We'll have to outthink him.>

<Head for the Coast Guard boat!> Tobias suggested. <We'll get beneath it and stay with it. The sound of the screws will keep him away.>

<Good idea,> Jake said.

We turned sharply and raced for the boat. It wasn't going to be easy. We needed to get beneath a boat that wasn't all that big while it was rising and falling on the waves. Besides, we were air breathers. We had to surface to get air, and couldn't hide there forever.

But it seemed to make sense. And would probably have worked. Except for one terrible fact.

<Ha-ha-ha, you think the propeller sounds will scare me off?> the killer whale said. <Nice try.>

CHAPTER 17

Six thought-speak voices said the identical word at the same time.

<David!>

<Yes, David,> he said with grim satisfaction. <Five little dolphins and one big orca. Let's see how that works out.>

<He still thinks Tobias is dead,> I said in private thought-speak. <He hasn't counted us. Tobias, stay behind us and —>

Ax interrupted. <David doesn't know which of us is Tobias. He's expecting five of us. We are six. The sixth person, the one who conceals his presence, could be any of us.>

<What are you suggesting?> Jake asked him.

<I am wondering, Prince Jake, whether one of us has a morph that could defeat David.>

<I do,> Cassie said.

<Okay, then, Ax is right. Cassie, hang back. Get out of range. Good idea, Ax. But don't call me "prince.">

<Yes, Prince Jake.>

<Okay, we need to keep David busy,> Jake said.

<Let's do it!> I yelled. I didn't care if David was ten times my size. I hated the creep. But the more sensible parts of my brain could not imagine how I was going to fight him and last more than a few seconds. Not as a dolphin, at least. Even a shark would be helpless. The orca was just too big.

<Hey, I'm Free Willy,> David said with a laugh. <Free Willy's hungry.>

<Why don't you tell that joke to Visser Three?> I sneered. <Maybe he'll arrange for you to die laughing.>

<Ah, Rachel. That is you, right? Psycho Rachel?>

<I'm the psycho? That's good, coming from a certified nutcase like you, David.>

<I'm nuts? Hey, I'm not the one threatening to kill anyone's parents, you crazy witch.>

There it was. Blurted out for all the others to hear. <I didn't threaten your parents,> I lied.

<Yeah, you did,> he said, and even I could hear the ring of truth. <Did you know that, big Jake? Did you know that, Cassie, with all your moralizing? Did you know Rachel threatened to kill my parents? How about you, Andalite? Of course we know smart-mouth Marco would approve.>

No one said a thing. No one came to my defense.

I felt hollow all of a sudden. Like I could feel their silence as a big hole in my insides. Who were they to be judging me? Which of them hadn't done things they were ashamed of?

Was I ashamed? Was that what I was saying?

No time for all that now. David had kicked his tail into overdrive and he was coming at us like a train.

<Okay, here's the plan: Whoever he chases, the others come in and nail him. Aim for his eyes. They might be vulnerable,> Jake instructed.

I was still waiting for him to say something. Like maybe "It's okay, Rachel, no big deal." But nothing. Nothing! I wanted to scream at him: "Why did you let me go after David if you didn't think I was going to threaten him? You hypocrite!"

But there wasn't time for that. Because now I could see the black-and-white pattern racing at me out of the gloom. He was lit up by a flash of lightning. He looked like some weird cross between a cow and a bus.

But this creature had a very large mouth and a lot of teeth. And he was very, very fast. He was aiming straight for Ax.

<I'm right here, David,> I said, and gave a kick with my tail. He veered, changing course, and hurtled toward me.

I kicked hard and rocketed straight at him, like I was aiming for his nose.

Closer . . . Closer . . . CloserCloserCloser!

I turned my flippers and went straight up. Up-UpUp, skimming past David's blunt snout!

WHOOOSH! Out of the water, into rain and lightning. High as I could fly. I hung in midair, looked down as gravity grabbed me again, and right below me I saw the killer whale's open mouth.

Falling! Falling toward that open mouth!

<Nooooo!>

But David was slipping back, too. He hadn't had time to get himself ready. He was slipping back beneath the water, and I was falling toward him. . . .

SPLASH! I hit water, not teeth, and I kicked madly to get speed. Where was David? I couldn't see him!

Echolocate, Rachel. Come on, concentrate!

I fired a burst. The echo was instantaneous. He was behind me. I jerked left and the big black-and-white snout went barreling past.

From nowhere another dolphin appeared. It rammed David's right eye with its beak, then slid down beneath the great monster.

<Ahhh!> David cried. But he kept his focus on me. I couldn't believe how quickly he turned. How quickly he built up speed to come back after me.

This was impossible! I was playing tag and I was *it*.

I rolled over, belly up, reversed course and slid beneath him, crossing sideways, literally rubbing belly to belly. Then I came up his right side, halfway down his body, back behind the tall, graceful dorsal fin.

Now I was out of his sight. As long as I stayed right there with him, move for move, he wouldn't see me, let alone reach me.

But David wasn't content to play tag with me. He targeted the next dolphin he saw and I couldn't match his speed.

As his tail blew past, I clamped my jaw down on it.

Big mistake.

He whipped me up and down, up and down as he kicked. Teeth ripped out of my jaw. Dazed, I had to let go. Then he turned and came for me again. I tried to swim, but the whiplash motion had disoriented me.

All I saw was a huge, gaping jaw coming right for me. And I knew I could not escape.

The orca filled my entire range of vision. So big! So impossibly fast.

And then . . .

Well, then I saw what orcas must want to be when they grow up.

Not the twenty feet of the killer whale, more like forty or fifty feet. Not the four or five tons of the killer whale, more like fifty or sixty tons.

Almost extinct, almost wiped out at one point. But there were still humpback whales in the sea. And one of them was Cassie.

<Hi, David, it's me, Moby Cassie,> Cassie said. <Why don't you leave my friend Rachel alone?>

If David had known much about whales, he'd have known that the humpback was almost powerless against him. It had no teeth. Just baleen.

But I guess there's something about seeing a creature the size of a house coming after you that makes you want to leave the area.

David left. But not before calling back to me, <Later, Rachel. There'll be another time.>

CHAPTER 18

I flat-out was not going to school the next day. I just didn't care. I went home and fell into my bed with my clothes on and was out cold.

Way too early in the morning I heard voices downstairs. Somber, muted voices. No laughter. I didn't care. I went back to sleep.

Then Jordan came up and kicked my bed till I rolled over, face plastered with hair, eyes glued shut. "It'd better be good or you are going to wish you'd never been born!" I said.

"It's Saddler," Jordan said.

It took me several seconds to make sense of that. "Huh?"

"He's not doing very well, I guess. They think he's going to die."

Saddler. My cousin. Jake's cousin. Right. Yeah, now I remembered. He'd been hurt. He'd been moved to the children's hospital near us.

"Oh. That's too bad," I managed to mumble.

"That's all you can say? 'That's too bad'?"

Obviously I wasn't going back to sleep. I sat up. I tried to wake my brain up enough to think of the right things to say, but my head might as well have been stuffed with cotton balls.

"He's probably going to *die*," Jordan said again.

I began to realize what Jordan wanted. She felt bad. She felt scared. She wanted me to reassure her.

I made a "come here" motion with my hand and fought down a yawn. "Sit here," I said, patting the sheet beside me. "Look, it's a bad thing. It's about as bad a thing as there is. I mean, he's just a kid. His parents are going to be so messed up after this. I know how you feel."

"It's just so bogus," Jordan said. "I mean, he was just riding his bike and then, like, all of a sudden his whole life is maybe over."

I nodded. "Yeah. Life isn't fair."

Jordan rolled her eyes at me. She knows a dumb cliché when she hears one.

"Sorry," I said. "Look, bad stuff happens. Doesn't mean it's going to happen to you. Doesn't mean it's going to happen to me or Sarah or Mom or Dad."

"Yeah, but that's what's so weird and all. I mean, I feel like scum because I felt kind of glad it wasn't me. You know? It was like 'Whew! Close one!' But that's not right. I should just be sad. And I am. Only it's not just sadness. It's also, like, 'Glad it wasn't me!' And then I was all, like, 'I would never ride my bike like that.' You know, the guy who ran into him is saying Saddler just shot out into the street without looking. So I'm thinking Saddler got run over because he was stupid and careless. But that's not right, either."

"It's not right, but I think it's probably normal," I said. "I mean, you don't want to think it could happen to you. So you have to come up with excuses. Ways it could never happen to you. You end up blaming the person who got hurt. Because then you don't have to think about what if it was you it happened to. You even start getting mad at the person it happened to. Like 'How dare he drag me down into all this pit of darkness? How dare he get hurt and make me feel bad?'"

Jordan nodded. "That's just so wrong, though."

I shrugged. "Yeah, probably. But it's also how people are. You don't want to go around thinking,

'It could be me next. It could be my sister or mother or father.' You're going to do anything you can not to feel that way. You have to put up a wall between you and the fear. You have to cut yourself off from it, tell yourself you're safe. Bad stuff only happens to people who are careless or stupid or evil."

Jordan seemed to feel better. She even smiled. "Mom says we can stay home from school today. You know, in case . . ."

I made a face. "Talk about a bad reason to skip school."

"Yeah. Well, maybe he'll be okay."

"Yeah. It's like on *ER*. The doctors are always worrying, but then the patient survives."

"And if they're a cute girl they get to date Noah Wylie," Jordan said, laughing.

"Exactly. So don't write old Saddler off yet, okay?"

She left and I staggered, still half-blind from the sleep gunk in my eyes, to the bathroom. I splashed my face with cold water.

<Ooooh, I never realized you were so wise and all.>

I jumped straight up. I spun around. Search . . . search . . . search . . . nothing! Nothing in the shower. Nothing on the floor. Nothing on the ceiling.

I stood there, very, very awake. "What do you want, David?"

<I just wanted to hear your deep wisdom, Rachel,> he said. <What's the matter? Does it make you nervous having me around?>

I kept searching the room. Inside the medicine cabinet. Nothing! Then, slowly, with a creeping, crawling sensation of disgust, I realized. He could be anywhere. He could be . . . *on* me.

"Should I go get some flea powder?" I asked the empty bathroom. I tried to sound tough and indifferent. Like I wasn't scared.

<You have to put up a wall between you and the fear, Rachel,> he mocked. <You have to cut yourself off from it, tell yourself you're safe, Rachel. You have to tell yourself that bad stuff only happens to people who are careless or stupid or evil, Rachel.>

"What do you think you're accomplishing, David?" I asked.

<I'm sending you a message, Rachel,> he said with silky intensity. <See, I know where you live, Rachel. That's my message. You want to threaten me? I know where you live.>

I had to fight down the panic that was competing with rage in my head. I couldn't let him know he'd gotten to me. "My family isn't part of this."

<So you say.>

"Your parents are Controllers now. That makes them different."

<Are you a hundred percent sure that your mother and your sisters aren't Controllers?>

I swallowed hard. I had to remain calm. That was the point. I had to remain calm. If I blew up he'd know he had power over me. "You would go after little girls, you gutless piece of crap. You said you wouldn't hurt humans who weren't in morph. I always knew that was bull. A coward like you has no honor."

It was a pathetic, obvious ploy. Would he fall for it? It depended. How did David see himself?

<You want rules, Rachel? I'll give you rules: Give me the blue box and I'm gone. I'll go to some other city. I'll take what I need. I have the power! But I want that box!>

"What for, you idiot? You want to make more Animorphs? Why? So they can do to you what you're trying to do to us?"

I guess that made him think. I thought it might.

<Stay away from my family, Rachel. I'll stay away from yours. Just you and me. That's the deal. You and me.>

"I'll take that challenge," I said.

<Cool. Now, hey, go ahead and enjoy your shower.>

He was silent after that. He said nothing more. Maybe he was really gone.

But for the first time, I decided to skip my shower.

CHAPTER 19

I didn't feel even slightly safe till two hours had passed. That's how long David could stay in morph. After that, if he'd been a flea or a cockroach or whatever, he'd be stuck.

Two hours later to the minute, I arrived at Jake's house. There were extra cars in the driveway. I guess Saddler's family had come over.

Jake answered the door. I saw half a dozen people beyond him in the family room. They all looked like they were getting ready to go.

"Hi, Rachel," Jake said. "Did you come over to —"

I grabbed him by his shirt and yanked him outside onto the porch. I've never done anything like that to Jake. I shocked myself. I know I shocked him.

"David was in my house!" I hissed in his ear. "He was in my bathroom."

Jake looked puzzled. Then his eyes widened. "In morph?"

"Of course in morph. You think he'd come over and ask my mommy if I could come out to play?!" I was yelling.

"Calm down, Rachel, the whole family is here. We're all about to head to the hospital to see Saddler. Tom is here," he added with a significant look. Tom is a Controller.

I lowered my voice to an intense whisper. "He was in morph. He may have been a flea. He may have been on me. On me!"

Jake nodded warily. "Yeah. I guess we have to expect that kind of thing."

"He's made me his number-one target," I snapped. "Did you expect that?"

"What do you mean?"

"I mean it's personal between me and him. And I think you know *why* it's personal."

Jake shook his head. "Look, we all stand together, Rachel. You know that."

"Do I? Nice job of standing up for me before, Jake."

"When?"

"You know when," I said. "When David told everyone what had gone down between me and him and all I hear is the big, empty silence from Cassie and Tobias and all."

"It was a combat situation, Rachel. What did you expect me to do? Stop and explain to everyone that David was lying?"

I glared at Jake and just then his dad came out on the porch. "We need to get going, Jake. Hi, Rachel. Why don't you come with us?"

I don't know why, but I said, "Okay, yes."

Jake's dad closed the door again.

"You think David was lying?" I asked him.

Jake looked away. "It doesn't matter what I think, Rachel."

I laughed. "You know something, Jake, you are becoming a real leader. You even have the whole hypocrisy thing down." I started to walk away. "Tell your dad I changed my mind."

"Rachel." Jake trotted over to catch up to me. "What's bothering you?"

"What's bothering me? Aside from the fact I've never been so tired in my life? Aside from the fact that David is out to get me? What's bothering me?"

"Yeah. Aside from those things. I mean, I know you, Rachel —"

"Yeah, you sure do," I snapped.

"Look, I don't have time for twenty questions."

"When you were going after David and you sent Ax for help, why did you tell him to get me and not Cassie or Marco?"

Jake looked surprised. He shrugged. "I don't know. I guess I thought you were closest."

"Wrong. Try again."

Jake flushed angrily. But then I saw the beginning of a rueful smile. "I thought David had killed Tobias. I thought he might kill me. I wanted . . . firepower."

"I see. You wanted me for my morphs." It was a good answer. It could have almost been true. "Okay. So we come down to the second question: What did you think I would say to David yesterday? In the cafeteria. Why did you let me go after him?"

Jake's rueful smile became sadder. For a long time he didn't speak. "I guess —"

"Jake! Come on. Rachel, if you're coming, let's go!" Jake's mom yelled.

At the same time the garage door opened and the family's new minivan came backing out. I piled in with Jake and there was nothing more said.

Maybe it was true about the morphs. Maybe I had jumped to a conclusion. After all, it was true

I had the grizzly bear morph and the elephant morph. Both of which were as strong or stronger than David's lion. And it was true that neither Marco nor Cassie had anything to match the lion's raw power.

Maybe that was all there was to it. Maybe my cousin didn't see me as some crazed *Femme Nikita* killer.

But I'd have to wait and hear his answer to my second question.

Jake had said, "It was a combat situation, Rachel. What did you expect me to do? Stop and explain to everyone that David was lying?"

But I knew one thing for sure: Jake was lying. He knew what David had accused me of was true.

Not for the first time, I looked at Jake and wondered what he had become. He was sitting there, looking like any other kid stuck in any other boring minivan. If you saw him walk down the street you might think, *Oh, there's a nice-looking guy.* But you wouldn't see half of what there was to Jake.

But then, I guess that's true of everyone. You can never be sure whether the pretty blond lugging a pair of bulging Express bags through the mall is just another sweet, ditzy, harmless mall rat.

Or me.

CHAPTER 20

You think hospitals are depressing? Try a children's hospital. You go to a regular hospital and see sick people and you think, *Oh, that's something that happens to old people.* You know, like lung cancer or Alzheimer's or whatever.

But in a kids' hospital you see way too many people who look like they could be sitting next to you on the school bus. It makes you nervous.

Saddler was in PICU. Pediatrics Intensive Care Unit. It was like the hospital room from hell.

Four beds in each room, if you can call it a bed when there are these monitors poised over your head showing your heartbeat and brain waves and a bunch of other stuff in wavy, ghostly green lines.

Three of the beds were full. Saddler was in the one farthest from the door. I took one look at him and thought, *Okay, I believe in mercy killing.* No one should have to be so . . . helpless.

But I guess that was dumb, because later I heard from one of the doctors that more than ninety-five percent of even the most messed-up kids who go into the PICU come out alive.

No one was being that optimistic about Saddler, though. He was going to be one of the five percent. At least that had been the last thing we heard from the doctors.

Now . . . well, let me just say that different people react in different ways to "miracles." We almost couldn't get to Saddler's bed for all the doctors and nurses crowding around. Some looked like they'd just had Leonardo DiCaprio tell them they were pretty. They looked transfigured. Others looked mad. Some looked scared.

Saddler's mother rushed to the head doctor. "Doctor Kaehler? What's happening? What's happening to my baby?"

Doctor Kaehler was one of the mad ones. "What's happening? Good question. Very good question. I have to tell you that we had a crisis here about an hour ago. Your son's heart stopped. We were rushing him to surgery, but in all honesty he was not going to make it."

"But —" she began.

The doctor ignored her. "I would have bet my entire career that Saddler would be gone within the hour. Then, as they were taking him up to the O.R., something happened with the elevator. It jammed or . . . or something. The nurse and doctor with him seem to have been knocked out. When they came to, the elevator was working again. They rushed your son to surgery where he . . . where he . . . opened his eyes!"

"What?"

"He opened his eyes. And he said, 'Hi.'"

Saddler's mother lost it. She shoved wildly through the gaggle of nurses and doctors. And there she stopped, staring in disbelief at her son.

Saddler was sitting up in his bed. He looked as healthy as if he'd just stepped in from playing soccer.

"How?" Saddler's father asked.

The doctor just shook his head. "You tell me. There is apparently nothing wrong with your son. And I mean nothing. No broken bones — all healed. No internal injuries. No bruises, for crying out loud!"

He was mad. I could understand that. He was a scientist, basically. Scientists like to understand things.

"It's a miracle!" Jake's mom whispered.

"I don't even believe in miracles," Jake's dad said, "but this is a miracle. I mean, I saw him yesterday and he looked like raw hamburger."

Saddler's parents were all over their son. Hugging, kissing, jabbering on and on. It was a cool scene. Even I was feeling overwhelmed. Then I caught sight of Jake.

He was the only wallflower at the big party of celebration. He turned away, rage barely concealed on his face.

"What?" I whispered to him. "What's the matter?"

He said one word. And I knew what I'd been too blind to see. This was no miracle.

Jake said, "David."

CHAPTER 21

Jake and I stepped back from the crowd. No one noticed. No one cared. They had a miracle to witness.

"You think David morphed Saddler?" I asked Jake.

"I know he did. Days back, I mentioned Saddler to all of you. I saw his eyes kind of light up. I didn't think much of it at the time. Besides, we were kind of busy."

I nodded. "He needed a life. David's family are Controllers and he needed a place to go, to sleep, to eat. But it's just a morph. If he stays in it more than two hours at a time he's stuck, and he'll lose his morphing power permanently."

"All he has to do is go the bathroom, de-morph, remorph, and he's good for another two hours. And take a look at his parents. You think they're going to notice, or care, if Saddler is suddenly very different than he has been?"

He was right. Saddler's parents thought they were losing a son. Now he was back. Alive.

A miracle.

So maybe his memory was a little impaired. Maybe he didn't remember his friends or his favorite food. He'd be different, but that was to be expected, with what he'd gone through. And anyway, Saddler always had been a jerk. David should be able to play the role.

What could his family even possibly suspect him of? Being a morph? Obviously not. Then something awful occurred to me.

"Saddler . . . where's Saddler? The real one?"

Jake looked grim. "I guess we'll have to ask David, won't we?"

I looked at Saddler. There was a momentary gap in the gaggle around him. He saw us. We saw him. His look was pure triumph.

Then the wall of people closed around him again. I was not even slightly surprised when, an hour later, Saddler said he had to go to the bathroom. By himself. He was fine, perfectly fine. Everyone should stop worrying.

He passed deliberately by Jake and me.

"Cousin Jake! Cousin Rachel! I'm glad you're here. Really, really glad."

For a brief moment, no one else was within hearing.

"You won't get away with this," I said.

"I won't? I already have. And what are you two going to do? The real Saddler was toast. Now those nice people have their son back. So what are you going to do about it?" He started to walk away, then turned back, as if he had some funny secret to impart. "I'll take the blue box, cousins. Bring it to me. You have twenty-four hours. Starting now."

He laughed, loudly enough for all to hear. So they all laughed, too, giddy from the fact that unbearable tragedy had missed them.

Jake and I plastered smiles on our faces. But we both felt sick inside.

David had beaten us.

Jake and I left. We went out into the mostly empty hallway.

"Okay, we have to plan right now," Jake said.

"Plan what?"

"We are never going to know whether we're being watched by David or listened to by David from now on," Jake said. "Right now we know where he is. Right now we're safe."

"So what are you going to do? Give him the blue box?"

Jake's eyes flashed. "Never!"

I smiled, despite myself. "Okay. So?"

"So . . . I don't know. Do you have any ideas?"

I stopped smiling. "What do you mean?"

"I mean, what do you think we should do about him? About David."

A nurse came by and flashed an automatic smile. When she was gone I said, "Look, Jake, I don't know what you're getting at. And you know what? I don't think I like what you're thinking about me."

"What? What's that about?"

"You never answered me before, Jake. I want to know. When David left the cafeteria and I started after him, and Cassie said no and you said to let me go, what exactly did you think I would do or say to David?"

Jake nodded. "Oh. That's what this is about."

"Yeah, 'Oh, that's what this is about.' What did you expect me to do to David? Did you think I was going to kill him? Did you? Is that why you let me go after him? Is that why you sent Ax for me? Because you think I'm some kind of violent nut you can call in whenever you need some dirty work done?"

"Look, Rachel, every one of us has his strengths and his weaknesses."

"And my strength is being some kind of crazy killer?" I practically shrieked.

"I didn't say that."

"You didn't *not* say it!"

"Okay, fine, Rachel. You want to do this, fine. I think you're the bravest member of the group. I think in a bad fight I'd rather have you with me than anyone else. But yeah, Rachel, I think there's something pretty dark down inside you. I think you're the only one of us who would be disappointed if all this ended tomorrow. Cassie hates all this, Marco has personal reasons for being in this war, Ax just wants to go home and fight Yeerks with his own people, Tobias . . . who knows what Tobias wants anymore? But you, Rachel, you *love* it. It's what makes you so brave. It's what makes you so dangerous to the Yeerks."

I let his words blow past me. I heard them, I'd feel them later, but I didn't want to feel them right then.

"You did think I'd go kill David the other day. My God."

"No. I thought you'd scare him. I thought you'd say the things it took to scare him. I thought you'd say whatever you had to. And I thought that of any of us, David would be most likely to fear you."

An attendant pushed a wheeled bed slowly

past. I tried to look at myself the way Jake saw me. Was it true? Did I love this war?

"I worry about you, Rachel. More than any of the others except Tobias. I feel like this war is to you like booze is to an alcoholic. Like I don't know what will happen to you if it all ends someday. What are you going to do? Go back to being the world's greatest shopper? Go back to gymnastics and getting good grades?"

I laughed harshly. "You worry about me? What do you think you're going to do? Jake, you're a leader now. You make life-and-death decisions. All the time. You've learned to do that. And," I added bitterly, "you've learned to use people. You use them for their strengths and their weaknesses. Worry about me? Like when all this is over you'll go back to being a mediocre basketball player and a decent student? You're not even in high school yet and you're the most wanted person in the Yeerk Empire. Visser Three would trade his Blade ship for your head on a stick."

We both fell silent for a while. From inside there came the drifting sound of laughter. David was back from the bathroom. Demorphed, remorphed, and good for another two hours. He could keep that up for weeks, maybe years. At night he could demorph and sleep. In the dark he'd look enough like Saddler. At school he could demorph and remorph between periods, in the stalls of the boys' bathroom. No need to worry about clothing. He'd fit Saddler's.

The creep. The evil little creep.

My own emotions brought me back to the moment.

"I'm not going to lose it, Jake," I said, staring down at the polished linoleum. "Maybe you're right. Maybe I do kind of get off on it all. But I still know where the line is. And I won't cross it. I am not some kind of nut. I know what I'm doing."

Jake nodded. "I know you do. But everyone draws their own line. Cassie's is in one place. Marco's is somewhere else. Yours is in another. Mine . . ." He made a failed attempt at a smile. "For example, see, I used to think my line was drawn at using my friend, my cousin, to do my dirty work. Guess that turned out not to be true. Sorry, Rachel."

I have no idea why I did what happened next. Because I'm really not that kind of person. But I hugged Jake. And he hugged me back.

And then he whispered in my ear, "Okay, now let's figure out how we take this creep down."

"You know it, cousin," I said.

CHAPTER 22

"Jake and I went over every possibility," I said. "Nothing. Nothing at all. He has us cold."

I looked around at the others. It was a grim-looking little group there in the barn.

"What do you mean, he has us?" Marco said loudly. "That little creep has us beat? No way. We've been kicking Visser Three's butt all this time and we lose to that jerk? I don't think so."

"Look, I don't like it, either. But it's reality, okay?"

Jake held up one finger. "Fact number one: David has the same powers we have. Which means he's as hard to destroy as we are. And the Yeerks have tried very hard to destroy us. How are we going to succeed when the Yeerks have failed with all their forces and technology?"

Marco raised his eyebrows in grudging acceptance.

<Yes, that makes some sense,> Ax agreed.

Of course, Tobias had nothing to say because Tobias wasn't there. Tobias was away.

Jake continued. "Fact number two: David can sell us out to Visser Three. I don't think he wants to do that because David's not a complete idiot and he knows that any contact he has with Visser Three is likely to be very dangerous for him."

"I'm not so sure he's not an idiot," Marco said darkly. "I would just like to point out that I never liked that guy. I said from the start that any kid who kept a pet cobra was trouble."

"Goodie for you, Marco," I said.

"Fact three: David has now acquired a morph of Rachel's and my cousin Saddler. What am I going to do? Make my uncle and aunt lose their son again? Better to leave David with them. And best of all, they live out of town, so David would be out of our faces."

"I have a problem with that," Cassie said. "I have a problem with the idea that these people lose their son and get this completely different person instead. That seems sick to me. It seems wrong."

"It is wrong," I agreed. "But what's the alternative?"

Cassie shook her head slowly. "There's no *good* choice here. But you know what? As sad and awful as it is that your cousin died, that's natural and normal and part of life. Having some ghoulish fake version of Saddler still around makes me kind of sick to my stomach."

"Fact number four: We give David the blue box and he has what he cares about. I don't know what he intends to do with it. Maybe he'll create his own little group of Animorphs." Jake made a face like "could be."

"Yeah, right," Marco sneered. "Here's fact five: David killed Tobias. And we're going to reward him?"

I exploded. "Hey! You think we like this? You think I, personally, like this? I hate that creepazoid. I would destroy him . . . if I could. But facts are facts, unless you're completely crazy."

Marco sneered. "I never thought I'd see the day. Fearless Rachel, mighty Xena: Warrior Princess, humiliated by some kid. You're done for, Rachel. No one will ever be impressed by you again. You're a joke."

I leaped at him and grabbed him by the throat. "Don't push me, Marco," I hissed.

He just laughed. "You know, I'm glad about

this, at least," Marco said. "At least David shattered the myth of mighty Rachel. It's a good thing you did survive, because now you have to live with the fact that you got beaten by David. I guess maybe you're not Xena, after all. But David may just be Hercules."

I shoved Marco back and turned away from his mocking laughter.

"Okay, then," Jake said. "Here's what I propose to do. I'm going to tell David where he can find the box. One of us will go with him. He'll probably want that, anyway, so he can be sure it's not a trap. He'll probably ask for Cassie. She had the least trouble with him. Speaking of which, Cassie, you're the only one who knows where the blue box is hidden."

"Not to be egotistical or anything, but where I hid it, no one would ever find it. For one thing, I had Ax disassemble it."

"Say what?" Marco asked. "It breaks down?"

<Of course,> Ax said a little snippily. <It has component parts. Cassie asked me to reduce it to smaller components so that she could hide each piece separately.>

"And so that I could carry the parts in morph," Cassie said. "Rachel and I —"

"Wait a minute, Rachel knows where it's hidden, too?" Jake asked, frowning.

Cassie looked embarrassed. "I kind of was scared to hide it where I hid it and not have someone with me. I mean, we had to do rat morphs to get there. And it took several trips because I could only carry small components one at a time."

Jake laughed. "I should have known if I told you to hide something really well, it'd be hidden where no one would ever find it."

"Oh, it's hidden, all right, piece by piece," I affirmed.

Jake sighed. "Okay, then. I'll see David-slash-Saddler this evening. I'll bring him a rat to acquire."

"That won't be much of a stretch for David," Marco said sardonically. "He's already at least half rat."

"You're going to bring him a rat at the hospital?" Cassie asked.

"No, he and his family are at my house," Jake said. "Nothing's wrong with him, so the hospital let him go. He's actually staying in my room. His so-called parents have the guest room, and I'm on the couch."

"What, you didn't want to share a room with David?" Marco said.

"I don't want to share a planet with him," Jake said. "Although I'll tell you all one thing. I wish it had worked out with David. Whatever else you can say about him, he's smart, brave, and in-genious."

We all nodded in solemn agreement.

Yes, yes, he was smart. But was he smart enough? That we would find out.

CHAPTER 23

We left the job of contacting David up to Jake.

My job, along with Cassie, Ax, Marco, and Tobias, was to prepare. Preparation involved a lot of work. Hard, physical work.

"You're sure David was in the barn?" I asked Tobias for about the tenth time.

<I can't swear he was in the barn,> Tobias said. <All I can swear is that a golden eagle left Jake's house. It flew here. It landed behind that old toolshed of Cassie's. David emerged from the golden eagle. Then he morphed to rattlesnake and was last seen sidewinding toward the barn.>

"Rattlesnake," Marco said. "Interesting choice."

"Good choice," Cassie said. "They fit in. They don't look out of place in this environment. They are poisonous, have very good senses, move faster than a lot of snakes. If, say, some red-tailed hawk decided to try and eat him, he could use his fangs."

Tobias laughed. <He's not worried about red-tails. I'm dead, remember? When he was in eagle morph, he saw me. He just assumed I was an innocent hawk flying around.>

We went back to work. Tobias flew cover, staying up high enough to spot anyone who might be approaching. But we had chosen a pretty deserted area to make our preparations. There wasn't much chance of anyone surprising us.

And we knew David wasn't around. Jake had called me to confirm that he was impersonating Saddler and being fawned over and pampered at Jake's house.

Already, it seemed, David was adapting nicely to the role. His "family" would be taking him home.

"At least the weather is better," Marco said. "I'd hate to be dealing with rain right now."

"Yeah, it's a beautiful day," I agreed.

<Why do humans consider some days to be better than others?> Ax wondered. <And what, exactly defines a "beautiful" day?>

"Sunshine, no clouds or at least not too many

clouds," I offered. "Warm but not hot. Low humidity, because humidity does bad things to hair."

<But rain is necessary, is it not? So why do you consider it to be less than beautiful?>

We were chatting away like that as we worked. Chatting almost compulsively. No one wanted time to think. No one wanted to have time to reflect on what we were doing and what it would mean.

But of course the reality of it all crept into our conversation here and there, in bits and pieces.

Cassie said, "I feel so sorry for Saddler's parents."

"Yeah," I agreed.

"I don't know how they are going to —"

"Also," Marco interrupted pointedly, "sunny days are better because on sunny days girls wear shorts and, like, little short dresses or whatever. What do they call them? Those dresses that have, like, straps on top and are usually yellow or whatever?"

"Sundresses?" I suggested.

"See? There you go: sundresses. As in sun. You don't hear about raindresses. You have rain*coats*. No one ever says, 'Whoa, you look excellent in that raincoat.'"

<These are types of artificial skin, I assume,> Ax said.

Even Ax was trying to keep the pointless blather going. Even he didn't want to think too much about what was happening. What would happen.

Tobias swooped low. <I think it's time I went and checked with Jake,> he said. <Ax-man? You need to get human if I'm not here to watch over you guys.>

<Yes, I will do that.>

Ax began to morph, changing from blue Andalite to olive-skinned human. Early on, Ax had acquired DNA from Jake, Cassie, Marco, and me in a process that allowed him to meld the DNA strands into one. The morph he was now adopting was a strange, and strangely beautiful, human male. I could look at him and literally see parts of myself in his face. Parts of the other fully human Animorphs, too.

One big advantage: With Ax in human morph, we wouldn't have to worry about obsessing over dark possibilities. Ax in human morph kept you busy.

See, Andalites don't have mouths. They don't make words and they don't have a sense of taste. Those two things have a tendency to overtake Ax's usual reserve and intelligence.

"These are good hands for working," Ax said. "Wurrr King. I am wurrr king. With hands-zuh. They are strong. Strong hands-zuh."

Marco sighed. "Here we go again-uh with the Ax-man doing his *Rain Man* impersonation."

I laughed. "Just be glad there's no chocolate around."

"Or nachos," Cassie added.

"Or cinnamon buns," Marco said.

Ax's handsome human head snapped around. "Cinnamon buns-zuh?"

"No, no, Ax. I'm pretty sure there aren't any cinnamon buns-zuh . . . I mean cinnamon buns . . . around here."

At last it was time to add the final piece to our creation. Ax and Marco screwed it into place. Marco tested the moveable part.

"That should work," he said, looking up at me.

"It better work," I said. "Because as awful as this is, the only alternative is worse. It has to work. It has to work or we . . . *all* of us," I added with emphasis, "we will have to become killers."

CHAPTER 24

David had chosen the ground for our meeting. A public place. Somewhere none of us could morph. It was inside a crowded Taco Bell.

Outside, night was falling. The neon signs were on. Most drivers had their lights on. The weather had turned bad again. Nothing like the storm the other night, but dark clouds that brought the night earlier than normal.

Inside it was all blazing lights and plastic seats and kids scarfing soft tacos.

The terms were that each of us had to be visible. But even now we weren't going to appear to be some kind of clique or whatever. Marco was with Cassie. Ax, in human morph, was with me.

Jake loitered around the counter, looking like he couldn't quite decide what to order.

The bright, public nature of the place was supposed to reassure us, too, I guess. We were supposed to be relaxed, not thinking it could be a trap.

But I'll tell you something. If Visser Three thought for certain that he could catch the "Andalite Bandits," as he thought of us, he wouldn't let the public get in his way. He wouldn't need to send in the Hork-Bajir. He could machine-gun the place using human-Controllers.

That would have made the news, but no one would have thought it was all that strange. I guess that says something about the condition of the human race, with or without aliens.

I sat there, watching Ax eat. I had started out hungry. But watching Ax tear through tacos, burritos, nachos, refried beans, packets of hot sauce and the bag they all came in . . . well, that kind of took care of my appetite.

"Spicy, right? This flavor . . . ver ver . . . this flavor is called 'spicy'?"

"Yeah. Spicy. Hot, too."

"Yes, it is hot."

"No, I mean the flavor is hot. So is the temperature . . . skip it."

"Skip?"

"Forget it. Let it go. Drop it."

126

No sooner were those last words out of my mouth than I regretted them. Ax promptly dropped the container of refried beans he'd been holding. It landed wrong side down on the table.

I didn't even have the energy to roll my eyes. I just went back to staring at the doors, slowly shifting my gaze from one to the next.

Then there he was. Saddler. David.

He swaggered in like he owned the world and everything in it. I so wanted to wipe that smirk off his face. But that wasn't in the script. My role was to seem chastised, beaten down. Defeated and humiliated. That's what we figured he'd want. That's what would make him happy.

David smirked at Jake. Then he brushed past him and came over to sit down across from me. "You can leave," he told Ax. "This is a humans-only section."

Ax turned his head awkwardly to look at Jake. Jake nodded. Ax got up and left. Jake took his place, sliding in next to David.

"So," David said, "we meet again, Rachel."

"Excuse me. I'm not involved in this," I said. I started to get up to leave.

David reached across and grabbed my arm. "What's the matter, Rachel? You don't like me?"

"Rachel's not involved, David. It's Cassie who hid the box. She'll show you where it is."

"I don't think so," David said. "I think Rachel is the guide I want."

"She doesn't know the way."

David laughed. He laughed exactly like Saddler. "That's a lie. Rachel knows."

"No, I don't," I said weakly.

"Don't be an idiot, Rachel!" Jake fumed. "David knows. He must have been in the barn." Jake looked like he was suddenly furious at the beans Ax had left behind. He swiped at them with his hand. A couple of globules of the brown goo landed on my arm.

Jake did not apologize. He just glared at me balefully.

David leaned forward, suddenly all business. "Okay, here's the deal. Rachel takes me to the box. And all of you will follow, staying back at least a thousand feet."

"You want us to follow you?" Jake asked incredulously.

"Of course. How else will I know where you are?"

Jake made a show of looking confused.

"Rachel will lead me to the blue box. You will each be there, right where I can see you, out of morph. Then Rachel and I go in, get the box, and we all say a tearful farewell. You go on fighting Yeerks, I go get rich."

Jake nodded.

But I said, "I can't go in there with him. I don't trust him! He could —"

"Rachel," Jake said, dripping disgust, "you know, I always thought there was a coward hiding deep down inside all that tough talk of yours. Just do it. You want to remain an Animorph? You'll follow orders."

I nodded, meek and afraid.

David searched my face through Saddler's eyes. Was he suspicious? Had I overplayed my part?

Then he reached across and smeared the re-fried beans down the sleeve of my shirt. And laughed.

So I did something I don't do much. I started to cry.

CHAPTER 25

David and I flew. He was in golden eagle morph, and I was in seagull morph. He kept me out in front. He followed close behind. If he had decided to attack me, I would have been helpless. I was like some little Cessna flying with a 747 behind me.

I led the way to the construction site. The construction site where everything had begun so long ago. Where Elfangor had given us our powers.

It was also the place where David had found the blue box.

<Aaah, yes,> he said. <Of course. The last place I would have looked for it. You put it back where it started out.>

I said nothing. I just flew. Jake, Cassie, Ax, and Marco followed at a distance.

I led the way down to one of the several unfinished buildings. It was just four cinder-block walls with a few doorless doorways. I think it was originally going to be a convenience store before the whole thing got canceled. Or maybe a fast-food place. Who knows? It didn't matter.

We landed in the center of the open, desolate enclosure. There were beer bottles and Coke cans strewn around. There was construction debris, weathered from long exposure to the elements.

<Stay in morph,> David ordered.

I did what he told me. I saw him begin to change, watching the brown feathers melt into pink flesh and the fabric of his morphing outfit.

I saw the moment when David's smirk emerged from the long, hooked beak. Glancing up, I saw the others circling overhead, doing as they'd been told. The darkness was spreading. My friends were fuzzy gray shadows against the darker clouds.

"Now, Rachel, now you can demorph. But as soon as you do, I want you to go into the rat morph we'll both be using."

I didn't bother answering. I just did what I was told. As I changed, David said, "You know, Rachel, it's a shame it worked out this way. I mean, if you weren't such a harsh person I would have invited you to quit this little gang and hook up with me. Jake doesn't even know how to use his powers. I mean, come on, who cares if the Yeerks are around? With Animorph powers we can have anything we want."

I began to change into the rat. It was a morph I'd done once before with Cassie. It was not something I wanted to do again. But David had to believe I had morphed it to help Cassie hide the pieces of the blue box.

I began to shrink. The fast, ever falling, falling, falling shrink you do when you're getting very small.

White fur rippled across my body. Down my arms, up my neck, down my back, itching against my outer clothing.

The concrete floor was rushing up at me. All the barely visible cracks and crevices in the concrete now looked like ditches and dried creek beds. The empty beer bottles loomed as big as buses.

My own legs were shrinking, becoming stubby, squat, shuffling things. My arms did the same. I could no longer stand. I fell forward.

I shriveled and shrank and became hideous as David seemed to grow ever more huge. He was a monster a million miles tall!

My face bulged out impossibly far, narrowing

down to a sniffing pink nose. My ears crawled up the side of my head. And from the base of my spine I felt the distant, numbed sensation of the long, hairless, ugly tail sprouting.

David began to morph, but I could not make it out for a while. Not till I saw the diamond-patterned scales ripple and replace his skin. Then his arms and legs began to dwindle away to smoke, and I knew for sure.

He was morphing the rattlesnake.

He was smaller and smaller, but as he morphed, he slithered his coils around me. Brown and tan and black coils looped around me, a fence twice, three times my height.

Sliding over the coils, the head appeared. A forked tongue as long as I was whipped out, tasted the air, and shot back in.

<One wrong move, Rachel,> David said. <Just one wrong move . . .> Then in "loud" thought-speak, he told the others to come down.

Down they came, spiraling through the last gasp of sunlight to land atop the walls that surrounded us. A falcon, a harrier, two ospreys. All deadly enemies of a rat.

<Now, all four of you demorph. One wrong move and I bite this rat here.>

He opened his fleshy jaws, revealed the hollow, poison-delivering teeth, and moved to within an inch of me.

I knew the rat was fast. But not faster than a striking rattler.

I was completely and entirely in his power. And I was afraid.

I was afraid. But the rat, surrounded by birds of prey and with its ancestral enemy the snake just a breath away, was in a state of shrieking terror.

CHAPTER 26

<Now, all of you demorph. As soon as you've demorphed, remorph,> David instructed.

<What morph?> Jake demanded.

<Cockroach.>

<That's not part of the plan!> Jake yelled.

<Too bad. You think I'm some kind of an idiot? You think I'm going to go into rat morph and have the four of you waiting around to squash me like a bug? Not a chance.>

<That's it, deal's done,> Jake said.

<Oh, yeah? Then you're going to lose another cousin, Jake,> David said. <You are all going to morph to cockroach. Period. And if there's no deal, I bite Rachel right here and now.>

I knew logically that Jake would go along. I knew that as a human. But the rat brain inside my own mind only sensed greater peril. Suddenly, the rat's body froze. Froze stiff with terror. I could not move a muscle. All I could do was quiver.

<I want your word,> Jake said weakly.

<You have my word, Jake,> David said generously.

It took ten minutes for the others to demorph and remorph. Soon four cockroaches scurried just beyond the snake's coils.

Then David demorphed.

I knew what was coming next. We all knew what was coming next. Still, it wasn't easy to act the part we had to act.

<So far, so good,> Jake whispered to me.

<Yeah. Let's just hope he doesn't go nuts on us,> I said.

<Cassie thinks he'll play it out the way we think he will,> Jake said.

I would have smiled if I'd had lips. Jake has a lot of respect for Cassie's ability to "read" people. So do I. Although, I reminded myself, Cassie had not seen how evil David could be.

<In any case, we do have a backup plan if he starts stomping us all,> I said.

<Not a great backup plan,> Marco said morbidly. <More like a really pathetic backup plan.>

David loomed larger and larger as he sprouted back into his human form. I saw him reach down and scoop up what could have been a beer bottle. He rummaged and found a cap.

<Here we go,> I told Jake and the others.

<What's he got?>

<Like we planned: a bottle.>

<Beer or soft drink?> Cassie wondered.

<Looks like Pepsi.>

<I guess that's good,> Marco said.

<Do cockroaches have a sense of taste?> Ax wondered.

David reached down and scooped up one of the four cockroaches. He put the mouth of the bottle beneath it and dropped it into the bottle.

<Hey! Hey, what's happening?> Marco yelled.

David laughed. "I'm putting you somewhere safe."

<What are you doing?!> Jake yelled.

"Don't worry, I'll keep my word," David said. "I'm not going to hurt any of you. I just want to make sure you don't hurt me. Now stand still and we can get this over with."

One by one, David scooped up my friends and dropped them into the Pepsi bottle. Then he screwed the bottle top back in place.

"Now, Rachel, we go get the blue box," David said. "Now that there's no chance of your friends interfering."

I saw four brown cockroaches trapped within the bottle. There was no way they could demorph. If one of them tried he would begin by crushing the others and would then be smothered within the bottle, ending up as nothing but a blob of unformed flesh.

David lifted the bottle up to eye level and laughed. "I've done what Visser Three and all his Yeerk Empire couldn't do! I have the Animorphs! Trapped! Hah-hah-hah!"

<You don't have the blue box yet,> I reminded him.

"But I will, Rachel. I will if you expect to see any of these friends of yours alive again. Yeah, I will have the blue box."

Cassie started screaming. <We'll be trapped as cockroaches! We'll be trapped forever!>

David sat the bottle down.

"Two hours, Rachel. Two hours till they are trapped forever as roaches. Let's go get that blue box."

CHAPTER 27

In the concrete floor of the never-to-be-finished building was a drain. The drain cover was off. Scurrying on rat feet, I led David to it.

It was about six inches in diameter. To a rat it was plenty big.

<Down there?> David asked nervously.

<Down there,> I said.

<You go first,> he said.

I nosed over the edge and blinked blindly at the darkness. I took a deep breath. At least it was better than the time I'd had to morph a mole and dig through the dirt. Not much better, though.

I dove over the side and into the pipe. I landed hard after a six-inch drop onto damp, rotting leaves and filth. I was expecting it. I had tested the route with Cassie earlier.

I quickly scurried a few inches down a horizontal pipe. David made a satisfying splat as he hit face first.

<Aaahh!>

<Watch out for that first step,> I said.

<I can't see anything!>

<Well, that would be because we're in a pipe underground,> I said.

<Don't make me mad, Rachel,> David said ominously.

<First piece is down this pipe,> I said. I scurried off, utterly blind, with David bringing up the rear.

<This better not be a trap,> David said. <You mess with me, I'll make sure you never get out of here. And your friends will spend the rest of their lives afraid of bug spray.>

<So what are you going to do with the blue box?> I asked.

<What do you care?>

<Just curious,> I said meekly.

<I'll need some people to help me. Like a gang.>

<Aren't you afraid that once you give someone morphing power they'll turn out to be a . . . to do what you did to us?>

David laughed. <You don't think I already

thought of that? You guys made a big mistake: You got me. See, I was smarter than any of you. That's why you lost. I'll be more careful. I'll only choose the kind of guys who are too dumb to do anything except obey me.>

I rolled my little rat eyes. This guy's ego just kept growing.

<Here's the first piece,> I said.

<Where?>

<Squeeze up here and you can feel it.>

<How do we get out of here with the piece?>

<Back up. There's a side pipe we can use as a turnaround.>

<Okay. You drag the piece.>

I grabbed the piece with my sharp little teeth and scooted backward, running occasionally into David's nose. Served him right.

We found the side pipe and awkwardly turned around.

<Where's the next piece?>

<Right down that side pipe. But we have to drag this one out first,> I said.

<Why? Why not get all the pieces and then push them all back to the exit pipe?>

<I . . . I guess we never thought of that,> I said.

<Of course not,> he said condescendingly. <But it's kind of obvious, don't you think?>

<Yeah. I guess it is.>

141

<Lead the way.>

I headed down the second pipe. Now my heart was really pounding. So hard I thought David might hear it and begin to suspect.

But no, I had carefully fed his bloated ego, and I had played the role of the beaten-down, humiliated girl. His guard was down. He'd killed Tobias. He had my friends trapped. What was there to be afraid of?

<Everything ready?> I called in private thought-speak.

<Everything is ready,> Cassie answered in a tortured voice. <May I be forgiven for what I am about to do.>

CHAPTER 28

Down the pipe. Through muck and standing water and filth. Past bugs of several types.

Down the black, claustrophobic tunnel. With David literally stepping on my tail.

I was close. Very close.

Fresh air! No! No! David would sense it, he'd realize . . . distraction! I had to distract him.

The pipe suddenly opened into what felt to us like a cavern. It was perhaps a foot square, steel all around, but the smell of fresh air was unmistakable to my sensitive rat's nose.

To my utter horror, I heard the sound of a distant jet flying overhead. There was no way we should have been able to hear that jet.

<What's that?> David demanded. <That sound, what is that sound?>

<Water in the pipes?> I suggested nonchalantly.

David pushed into the chamber beside me. All I had to do was back out, get back down that pipe before he did. But if I lunged he would know instantly.

<Smells different in here,> he said.

<Yeah, it does,> I agreed.

Neither of us could see the other. But I could almost hear the wheels turning in his head.

A sudden sound of movement!

He knew! He was going for the exit.

I jumped to block his path. Damp fur against damp fur, we collided. In a flash he was on me, teeth and paws tearing at my face.

<You think you can trick me?!> he shrieked.

We fell back, face-to-face, both bleeding. The pipe was on my right, on David's left. We were equally close to it. Equally far away. Both utterly blind.

<Be ready,> I told Jake grimly. <Be very, very ready. We have problems.>

David rushed at me, but this time I slid beneath his gnawing mouth, then jerked upward, throwing him off-balance.

I leaped for the exit.

Stopped!

He had my tail in his jaw. He was pulling me back. I couldn't reach him, and if I tried we'd go around in a circle like a dog chasing its tail. He'd be able to get back out of the pipe, maybe escape altogether in the sewer network.

<Have a good grip back there, Davey boy?> I said.

<You won't get away!>

<Yeah?> I twisted back, just as David hoped I would. Only I didn't attack him. Instead, ignoring the hideous pain, I chewed through my own tail.

<Aaaahhhh!> I cried in agony as the last shred of skin parted.

<Nooooo!> David screamed as he fell back, holding nothing but a few inches of tail.

I darted for the exit, and before I was halfway into it yelled, <NOW! NOW! NOW!>

The steel gate slammed down. It would have snagged my tail, if I'd still had one.

David slammed against the barrier. It was a dull thump.

<No! NOOOOO!>

Suddenly, there was light everywhere. A flashlight shone right on my face. I blinked like a miner coming up after a day digging coal.

<Hey, you want to point that somewhere else?> I grumped.

In the light of two wavering flashlights, everything could be seen. The way the ground above the pipe had been dug up, baring the pipe. The way the pipe had been cut. And the steel box that had been affixed to the pipe end.

Not to mention the sliding door that turned the box into a cage. A trap.

The top of the box hinged up. But there was a strong wire grid to keep David inside.

There he was, a rat. He blinked up at the faces around him: Jake, Cassie, Marco, Ax. And my face as I quickly demorphed.

<No way! How did you get out of that bottle?> he demanded.

That's when Tobias swooped down from the dark sky and landed atop the cage.

<But . . . but you're . . .>

<Dead?> Tobias supplied. <No. You killed some poor red-tail who was minding his own business. I broke the Pepsi bottle. The bottle we deliberately left where you could be inspired to use it.>

"See, David," Marco said, "we knew you were in the barn, listening to our every word. How did we know? Tobias. So we played out that whole pathetic scene for you about how disgraced Rachel was. We knew you'd get so much sick pleasure out of forcing her to obey you."

"That piece of the blue box we retrieved? A Lego," I said.

<All of your actions, even your emotions, were

anticipated,> Ax said. <We anticipated how you would respond. So we were able to manipulate you.>

<Okay, okay,> David said with a laugh. <Okay, so you guys won. That's cool. I can accept that. Fine, I'll go my own way now.>

No one said anything.

<Look, I'm serious, all right? Jake, you're the man, okay?>

I looked at Jake. He looked like he hated being alive. I turned my gaze to Marco. He was carefully staring into empty space.

Cassie was crying.

David hadn't asked who the mastermind of the plan was. Who it was who had so accurately appraised his emotions, his need to build his ego, the fact that he would choose me to be his "companion." Cassie, of course. Cassie had worked it out, step by step, after Jake and I failed to come up with anything.

For Cassie, it was an improvement over the alternatives. See, no one was going to have to die.

But David's life would end, just the same. And so would "Saddler's." Eventually, they would find the real Saddler's body, and then they would know, that at least for them, there was no such thing as a miracle.

<No,> David whispered as the truth began to dawn on him. <No, no. No.>

None of us had a watch, of course, since we'd morphed. But Ax was very accurate about keeping track of time.

Jake looked at Ax. Ax showed no visible emotion. But I knew Ax well enough to know that he was not exactly enjoying any part of this.

<He has been in morph for thirteen minutes,> Ax reported.

<No, no, no. You guys aren't going to do this!> David cried.

"You tried to kill us," Jake said. "You threatened to turn us over to Visser Three. Not to mention what you've done to Saddler's family."

<You can't judge me!> David cried. <You're not God!>

"David, we have fought the Yeerks for a long time now. It seems like forever," Jake said wearily. "We are not going to let you beat us. We are going to save the human race if we can. There are larger issues . . . more important . . ."

Jake looked at Cassie helplessly. He shrugged and made a face like he couldn't stand hearing himself talk.

"We're doing to you what you were trying to do to us," I said. "Law of the jungle: eat or be eaten."

I looked at the others. "No need for all of us to hang around here. It looks too obvious. It's bad security. I can handle this."

<I will stay, to keep track of the time,> Ax said.

I nodded.

"You don't have to do this, Rachel," Jake said. "Everyone is in on this. We all made this choice."

"Yeah, but it won't bother me. It will bother you guys."

Of course Jake didn't believe me. Neither did Cassie or Tobias. Maybe Marco did. I don't know.

No one made a move to leave.

"Look, get out of here!" I roared. "Get out of here! You're just drawing attention. What if someone comes by? Get out of here!"

Jake nodded. "Yeah," was all he said.

Jake's a good leader. He knows when to use us. He knows when to protect us. He knew he had to protect as many of his people as he could from what was going to happen.

He took Cassie's arm and called to Tobias and Marco.

<You can't do this,> David moaned. <You can't do this!>

<It is now fifteen minutes,> Ax said.

I closed my eyes and wished I could cover my ears to keep out the sounds. But it was thought-speak I was hearing. And you can't block that out.

CHAPTER 29

It took two hours for David to become a *nothlit*. A person trapped in morph.

Two hours. But that two hours of horror will last forever in my mind. If I live a hundred years, I will still hear his cries, his threats, his pleading, each night before sleep takes me. And beyond sleep, in my dreams.

Once we were sure he was trapped, Ax and I morphed. I morphed into bald eagle, Ax into harrier. We took turns carrying the helpless rat out across the beach, across the breaking surf, out to the tiny, desolate rock a mile or more from shore.

There were other rats there. Guess there had

to be a food supply. But the rocks and the waves kept humans away from the place.

We left him there. And we flew away.

<Rachel?> Ax said.

<Yeah?>

<I think . . . I think I will never want to speak of this again.>

I didn't answer. I was still listening to the thought-speak cries that followed us for so long. That long, wailing, <Nooooo!>

At last, the cries were left behind us.

We flew over the Marriott resort where the summit meeting had taken place. It still looked pretty bad. There were repair crews everywhere. No sign of the world leaders.

Maybe they'd decided to take the meeting somewhere else. I can't even imagine what they made of the whole thing. Hard to explain being attacked by elephants and rhinoceroses here in . . . well, never mind where "here" is.

Something kind of snapped in me after that. I didn't suddenly become all soft and mushy or anything. I didn't turn into a wimp. But somehow the joy I'd gotten from combat, the thrill I'd gotten from battle against impossible odds . . . well, I guess maybe I just grew up a little.

We never heard from David again. Not directly, at least. But months later I heard some kid at school talking about the rock.

It was haunted, he said. He and his family had passed close by on a boat. He swears he'd heard a faint, ragged voice crying, "No! No!"

#23 The Pretender

"Hello. My name is Tobias. I . . ."

I hesitated. The secretary was looking at me skeptically. Like maybe I'd come in looking to borrow a quarter for the video game at the convenience store.

"My name is Tobias." I told her my last name. Weird. I could barely remember it. It felt like I was using an alias. "I think Mr. DeGroot wanted to talk to me."

She was puzzled. I looked at her nameplate. Ingrid.

"It's pronounced DeGroot. It rhymes with boat."

"Oh."

"Let me just check with Mr. DeGroot." She picked up her phone and punched a line. "Mr. DeGroot, there's a young boy named Tobias —— out here. He says — oh. All right."

She hung up the phone.

"I guess he does want to see you," she admitted. "Right through that door."

I checked the door. Fine. The lawyer's office was still sharing a wall with the laundromat. If I started yelling it would take Rachel about three minutes to morph and come through that wall.

Three minutes is a very long time when you can't even fly.

I used the doorknob. Yes, human hands were very cool. As a bird I'd have been totally defeated by a doorknob.

DeGroot was younger than I'd expected. More in his twenties or thirties than really old. He was wearing a white shirt and red suspenders. His jacket was thrown casually over a chair.

He jumped up and smiled.

"So, *you* are Tobias."

"Yes. I'm Tobias."

He looked me up and down. I did the same to him.

"I've been hoping I could locate you, Tobias. Have a seat, please. Would you like some water? A soda? Coffee? No, I guess you don't drink coffee at your age. A soda? We have Coke, diet Coke. And we might have some Dr. Brown's cream soda. I'd have to have Ingrid check."

If he was getting ready to pull a gun and shoot

me, or expecting to have Visser Three come storming in the door, he hid it very well.

I relaxed a little. But I was baffled. Water? Coffee? Soda? What was the right answer?

"Um . . . um . . ."

Good grief. You'd think it was Final Jeopardy and the category was Obscure Modern Poets. I was so out of practice being human.

"I'd like a Coke!" I practically yelled.

DeGroot pressed his intercom. "Ingrid, our young friend would like —"

"— a Coke. Yes, I heard him. All the way out here."

The lawyer and I stared at each other till the Coke came. I gripped the can self-consciously and pressed it to my beak. Lips.

It had been a long time since I'd tasted sugar. I almost burst out laughing. It was like being Ax in human morph. The taste of sugar was overwhelming! And the coldness. I hadn't felt cold in my mouth in a very long time.

"Tobias, where have you been staying? Your legal guardians both seemed to think the other one had you."

Not a question I wanted to answer. "I take care of myself."

DeGroot smiled. "No doubt. But you are under age. You can't 'take care of yourself.' Not legally."

"You can't lock me up," I said. Literally true. One thing about being an Animorph: No home, no building, no school, no jail or prison could hold me.

The lawyer looked pained. "That's not what I am talking about."

"Okay. What are you talking about?"

That seemed to set him back a little. It was weird. I had a toughness I'd never had when I was human. As a human I'd been a bully magnet.

"Here's the thing. I represent your father's estate."

"My father is dead." That's what I told him. But over the years and especially lately I'd begun to wonder.

"Tobias . . ." He leaned across his desk. "Your father, that father, the man who died? That may not have been your *real* father."

"What?"

"I have a document . . . it's a strange situation. Very strange. Look, Tobias, I'm going to level with you. My father used to run this office. He's dead, too. He left this document along with the rest of his clients' papers. But on this he wrote me specific instructions. Very specific. On the date of your next birthday your father's last statement was to be read to you, if at all humanly possible."

I didn't know what to say. If this was a trap, it was a weird one.

"Are you okay? You don't seem surprised."

No, I didn't, I realized with a start. I had forgotten to make facial expressions. It was something I didn't do as a hawk.

"I am surprised," I said. I twisted my face into what I hoped was an expression of surprise. But it occurred to me that I was facing a new problem: He'd said he'd read the document on my next birthday.

When was my birthday? I couldn't exactly ask him.

"Now there's this new complication. A woman named Aria, who says she is your cousin. Your great-aunt's daughter. Apparently she's only just learned of your situation. She's a very acclaimed nature photographer and she's been on long-term assignment in Africa. She wants to meet you."

"Why?"

"You're family. She wants to help you."

"Oh."

"She'd like to meet you tomorrow. At the hotel where she's staying. If that's okay. It's the Hyatt downtown. Do you know where that is?"

I could have said, yes, I am familiar with their roof. A peregrine falcon has a nest there in a niche in the radio tower. And the thermals are great, sweeping up the south face of the building, warm air radiating up from the street below and gaining strength from the sunlight reflected off all those windows.

What I did say was, "Yeah, I know where it is."

"She's very concerned for you."

"Uh-huh."

"Do you need money? A place to spend the night?"

"No. I'm fine."

He shrugged doubtfully. "You look healthy enough. Well dressed."

I almost laughed. Rached had picked out my wardrobe. I looked like a poster boy for Tommy Hilfiger.

"I get by okay. Um . . . so when did you say you're going to read this document?"

"On your birthday."

"Ah. Okay. Bye."